A Flicker of Hope in the Age of

Artificial **I**llumination

By: A.R. Weston

Have you ever had a dream so real that waking up felt like the wrong ending?

- A.R. Weston

The Last Candlemaker: A Flicker of Hope in the Age of Artificial Illumination

www.arweston.com

ISBN: 978-1-949439-20-5

Content Disclaimer

This novel is a work of fiction and is allegorical, intended for entertainment purposes only. All events, institutions, technologies, systems, ideologies, and characters depicted herein are fictional and are not intended to represent or promote real-world political movements, belief systems, organizations, infrastructure, tactics, or technologies.

Any depictions of authoritarianism, persecution, violence, or social control are presented solely for narrative and thematic purposes and are not an endorsement of such actions or ideologies.

Any resemblance to real persons, living or dead, is purely coincidental. All character names, physical descriptions, personalities, behaviors, and dialogue are fictional and not intended to depict or reference any real individual.

References to "Artificial Illumination" and "AI" within this work are symbolic and metaphorical and should not be interpreted as commentary on real-world artificial intelligence systems, products, or government policies.

This work contains themes of societal oppression and implied harm, which may be disturbing to some readers. Reader discretion is advised.

Table of Contents

It started with the candlemakers.
Few noticed.
Fewer objected.
When it came for the rest,
it already had a name.

PART I

"The World Before it Breaks"

A Beautiful Light

It was March 22, 1884, and the city of Hanover lay under a darkness thicker than usual. Candles burned in every window in town. They illuminated church altars and were mounted on every street post.

Inside the Bliss Candle Factory, Chandler Bliss, fourth of his name and the youngest grandson of Earl Bliss Sr., looked out at the dim street before turning back to his bench. A candle burned in a glass jar beside him. The flame was straight and calm. It made him smile, a small thing, but enough to remind him why he loved his work. This flame didn't move much, and Chandler wondered why it bothered him.

"Another candle by candlelight," he whispered to himself. "Great-grandfather would be proud."

He reached into the warm bucket of wax and lifted out another handful. It yielded under his fingers the way it had since he was a boy, learning beside his father. His thumbs pressed slowly along the surface, shaping the taper the same way his family had done for generations.

The factory itself was a relic from the previous century, its brick walls browned by years of smoke and heat. Lanterns hung along the central hall, casting a warm haze over the long rows of benches. Every station had initials carved into the wood, some fresh, and some so old the letters had sunk deep into the grain.

Though the workers went home at night, the place never seemed still. Apprentices arrived long before dawn, fumbling with stiff fingers to open the stoves and ready the molds. The day started once the noise picked up. Someone would snap a wick-cutter too hard, a mold would drop on a table, and apprentices frequently yelped when they burned their fingers.

Chandler always came in earlier than anyone else. He liked the quiet before the day started, when the building felt solemn. He'd walk the central aisle, brushing his fingertips along the hanging tools and brass-handled ladles that had belonged to men long gone. Some had been carried across the Atlantic by the first Bliss candlemakers. Chandler knew every inch of the factory by memory. In the silence, he pictured the place the way his grandfather used to describe it.

He had a habit of beginning the day the same way, without fail. Before lighting the stoves or touching any wax, Chandler would stop at the small basin near the east wall and wash his hands. The water was always cold and fresh from the pump out back. He scrubbed deliberately, working away the grit from beneath his nails. Only when his hands were clean did he dry them on the same linen cloth his father had once used.

It wasn't about cleanliness, as the grit would return within moments of starting his work. The wax would coat them again soon enough. His morning routine was about preparation. After that, he would grab a single candle near his bench. He never used a new candle in the morning as it was bad luck. He inspected the used candle thoroughly, checking the wick with his thumb and forefinger. He'd set it into the glass jar beside his workstation.

Striking the match was its own small ceremony. Chandler liked hearing the sound it made against the lip of the table. The flame would sputter and then bloom in all its brilliance. He would hold the match still, watching it catch fully before presenting it to the wick.

"That's a beautiful light," his father used to say when he saw Chandler do this as a boy. "A well-made candle is a thing of art."

Chandler could still hear his father's words as if it were yesterday, though it had been years. He appreciated that candlemaking had mostly passed from father to son. Although the work was simple in appearance, the pride behind it ran deep. Every candle bore the touch of the man who shaped it, whether that reflected patience or carelessness.

Once he had completed his morning ritual, he waited just long enough to appreciate the flame. Only then did he begin his work for the day. He wasn't alone in this.

Most of the men had their own unique morning rituals. Samuel Roy, a candlemaker, who was built like a Clydesdale horse, always re-tied his boots, although they were already secure. Travis Cloud, a senior candlemaker, and a friend since childhood, prayed under his breath, then traced a cross over his chest. Travis was a tall, thin man whose beard always carried bits of wax hardened into the hairs. He was known for being a good man, but also for having a short temper.

Apprentices, still unsure of themselves, tended to copy whatever they saw their mentors do. It was common for them to blend one man's habit with another's until it became something they called their own. No one had to teach or force the men to complete morning rituals; they just did them.

Occasionally Chandler walked down the aisle after lighting his candle. He checked the tools as he went. If a ladle hung crooked, he straightened it. If a wick-cutter's blade was exposed, he closed it. He paused at the far end of the hall, looking out the narrow window at folks walking to work.

Hanover was quiet at that hour. The street posts glowed faintly against the pale morning mist. Lamp tenders were finishing their final rounds. Chandler watched them perform their work with flawless precision. They would come slowly and then disappear quickly around the corner.

"People will follow beautiful light," he said to himself, echoing his grandfather's words of truth.

He would spend more time than he should at the window, but would eventually return to his bench. He picked up the wax horse his grandfather had made long ago. He gently rubbed it with his hand and then set it back in its place. It was an imperfect artifact from the past, but it had survived fires, floods, and time itself.

Footsteps at the factory doors meant the apprentices had begun to arrive. They were not known for being quiet as they stomped eagerly through the door, throwing it open with a loud thud. Chandler took one last look at the candle burning beside him. The flame stood proudly, indifferent to the noise.

"Thank you for giving us light, my old friend," he whispered to the candle. The candle did not answer, of course, but this little phrase of reverence to the candle was a Bliss family tradition. Something in that small, steady flame reminded him that hope came from the One beyond any light a man could make.

By midmorning, faint rays of sun broke through the river mist and spilled through the film of soot on the windows. With the stoves lit, the place changed. The tallow started melting with a few sharp pops, always louder when someone hadn't cleaned the pot well. Chandler gave the rim a quick scrape with his ladle, more out of habit than anything.

Once the wax was ready, they poured it into the molds in steady ribbons. A clumsy splash could ruin a batch or burn a hand badly enough to prevent months of work, so the men moved slowly, acting with care. Making candles was not something that should be done hastily nor without thought.

Apprentices often paused to watch Chandler. His arms were thick from years of lifting crates, and his fingers looked built for heavier labor, yet the wax responded to his touch like soft clay. He intentionally mouthed bits of advice as he worked, not loudly, but loud enough for the boys hovering nearby to overhear. They tried to copy him, usually making a mess of their wax in the process, but he never scolded them.

By midafternoon, the place was loud enough a man had to raise his voice to be heard over the clatter. Molds opened with clacks and bangs. Warm candles dropped onto wooden tables, and apprentices called out when they finished their batches. Each apprentice hoped for and sought a nod of approval from their mentor. Above them, rows of fresh tapers swayed gently from the racks, chiming together whenever a breeze slipped in through the doors.

Every worker knew the one rule drilled into them since they started in the factory. Chandler learned this rule before he was taught his ABCs. It was a rule built on a simple premise: a candle could not be rushed to a flame. Wax cooled when it wanted to and wicks absorbed oil at their own pace. Even the nearby river's humidity could make or break a batch.

Young apprentices wiped sweat from their brows while older men settled comfortably into the warmth of the factory. Lunch for a seasoned candlemaker was bread, cheese, and whatever meat was left over from dinner the night before. The apprentices relied on butcher scraps and ate quickly so they could get back to making candles, all hoping to earn favor. Chandler often lingered an extra minute, enjoying his lunch, while observing the apprentices hustle back to their stations.

The hours after lunch slipped away. As the sun moved through the afternoon sky, its light mixed with the glow of hundreds of workshop candles. The final hours of work were Chandler's favorite. Today, though, the factory seemed different, but he couldn't explain why.

Change Without Trumpets

Here and there, thin trails of hardened wax snaked across the floorboards. The wax formed tiny ridges no broom could ever fully lift. Wooden molds smacked and clacked together as hot wax filled them. The candlemaker would follow the filling of the molds with a quick snip of the wick-cutter. To a banker or investor, it would have been obnoxious noise, but to a candlemaker, it was music.

A narrow loft overlooked the main hall. Chandler knew his great-grandfather had once stood there, watching the candlemakers below. The tall arched windows behind it were clouded by years of steam and smoke. The remaining strips of afternoon sunlight slipped through, catching the glow of the workroom candles.

For generations, the Bliss Candle Factory had produced all the candles for Hanover. All the candles for churches, manor houses, and even the lanterns carried down into the mines were a Bliss product. Near the central aisle of workbenches, a group of candlemakers had gathered between the racks of cooling tapers. The men spoke loud enough to cut through the hiss of melting wax.

"Did you hear about that shipment from Louisville?" asked Travis. "They're using some cheap new blend. I hear it's imported stuff that doesn't need a second mold."

"Imported wax snaps in the cold," another man shot back with a sarcastic response. "People buy Bliss because our candles don't crumble like old bones. Those *new* candles won't last a week."

"Maybe not," Travis said with a short laugh, "but cheap sells. People in Hanover will want to try it; they always do."

The conversation stalled, long enough for Chandler to notice that no one seemed eager to have the last word. He shaped a thick taper while he waited and listened. Rumors like this surfaced every few years, new methods, competitors, and factories trying shortcuts. That same factory in Louisville was known for cheap knockoffs.

"You worry too much," teased Samuel. "The Bliss name has weathered storms worse than this. Hanover wants quality, not cheap rubbish. Let other men make garbage candles if they want. We'll keep making candles worth buying."

"Quality doesn't mean much to men who can't afford bread," Travis crossed his arms.

Before the debate, which was gearing up for a fistfight, went any further, Earl Bliss Jr., Chandler's father, marched down the aisle. He walked with a determined pace, as if he wanted to look in charge. He wiped his hands on a cloth, though they were clean enough to suggest he'd done little work. His hair was slicked back, his pants and shirt neatly ironed. He was dressed like a man expecting company.

A thin stack of papers sat on the edge of the central worktable. Chandler had noticed them earlier but thought little of them. Earl Jr. paused to give them a quick look. They were city forms, stamped and neatly bound, delivered that morning by a courier from City Hall. The top page had a due date written in bold letters.

The Bliss Candle Factory was required to return the forms by the end of the day. The mayor of Hanover requested an updated staffing roster, projected monthly productivity, quantity of the materials used, and the total of last month's revenue. In addition, there were questions about worker morale, tenure of the staff, and their home addresses. At the bottom of the survey were the initials, **S.V.**

"Back to it, gentlemen," he ordered. "This isn't a tavern. Save your tough talk and fighting words for the pub."

A few men straightened up right away. A couple of men smirked, making rude faces once he passed them. Earl Jr. wanted to command the factory the way his father did, but authority wasn't something you inherited. It was earned with years of wax burns and long hours.

He stopped at Chandler's bench, nodding in approval. "Let's see… good taper, with even height, and a solid base. Your grandfather taught me the same technique, too!"

"Thank you, sir," Chandler earnestly replied, though Earl Jr.'s words felt patronizing. He respected his father, but he disliked him using praise as a way of propping himself up.

Behind them, the conversations resumed in lower, more guarded tones and reduced volume. Chandler caught pieces of it as he rolled another batch of warm wax, waiting for his father to move on to the next station. The men discussed growing cities, machines replacing labor, and strange new inventions being tested in places like New York and Philadelphia.

Several of the men went back and forth on a wide range of topics. A few made bold claims that the laborers of the nation needed to unite under one banner as they shared a common cause. One man, regarding Hanover's economy, paraphrased Marx, proclaiming, "A man ought to give what he can and, in return, take only what he needs to live." None of them understood the topics they were chatting about, but that didn't keep them from giving their opinion.

"The world's changing," Travis asserted. "You can feel it! Pretending otherwise is foolish!"

"Maybe," the other replied, "but people will always need light."

Chandler wanted to believe it, but something in him hesitated. Change didn't usually march in with trumpets and drums; it crept in unseen. The factory doors opened with a heavy groan. Earl Bliss Sr. stepped inside. At first, the men didn't seem to notice, or that was until Earl Sr. got within a few feet of them.

All conversation died without another word being spoken. His posture was rigid and his stride firm. Though his hands no longer bore the fresh calluses of daily labor, they were still the hands of a man who'd earned his place. He approached the cluster of workers and stood listening for a moment before they realized he was there.

"I heard something about cheap wax from Louisville," he said after a noticeable pause, his deep voice carrying easily across the hall.

"Yes, sir," Travis softly replied.

"You know what they say... those who are willing to trade quality for a few saved dollars," Earl Sr. said with a snort, "deserve to get what they pay for!"

Men throughout the factory nodded. Even Travis looked subdued. If that had been any other man speaking to him, he would have been ready to go fisticuffs. He stood there quietly as Earl Sr. continued.

"That said, we must not fool ourselves. Carriages improve, miners dig deeper, and presses print faster than they did yesterday," Earl Sr. took a deep breath. "New machines, faster ways to work, efficiency, and productivity... Hanover will not remain satisfied while the world moves forward."

His words were sharp, urgent, and felt rehearsed.

"The world is, in fact, changing," Earl Sr. declared, "and new ideas are spreading with it. We will honor our legacy, but we will strengthen it, as well."

A chorus of voices all came together. "Hear, hear!" a few men spoke as one. There was collective agreement passing through the group both verbally and with subtle facial expressions. Chandler, though, noticed something else in his grandfather's expression. Something felt off.

"Chandler, walk with me." Earl Sr. turned.

Chandler set down the unfinished taper and followed him to the quiet end of the hall where the windows overlooked the street. The workers drifted back to their stations as the rhythm of the factory resumed around them. Earl Sr. picked up a newly molded candle, turning and spinning it between his fingers.

"You love this work," he said.

"Yes, sir," Chandler replied. "I do."

"Your hands say as much," Earl Sr. pointed downward. "You care more for this craft than some of these men care for their own wives. That's not a skill; it's a gift, it's passion."

Chandler nodded.

"But..." Earl Sr. continued, "this isn't romance. It's a trade and a business. These men feed their families because this factory stands. Sentiment and passion don't keep the doors open. Only discipline does that." He set the candle back on the rack.

"One day the company may face changes you don't agree with. When it does, you can't let your heart cloud your judgment. A leader must bend without breaking." His expression softened. "I need to know you can do that, not as a boy fond of wax, but as a man leading the way."

"I'll do my best." Chandler swallowed.

"Your best? I suppose that's all a man can promise anyway." Earl Sr. patted Chandler's shoulder. "You'll make a fine leader someday, perhaps a great one. I will warn you though, greatness takes clarity. Always remember, the only constant in life is change."

He left Chandler standing alone. When Chandler returned to his bench, the men were talking again, though their voices lacked the bravado from earlier. Travis approached him without his normal bombastic demeanor.

“Are you alright?” he asked.

Chandler nodded, though he didn’t feel entirely sure. His grandfather’s words had weight, and they were neither comforting nor ominous, just heavy.

“All this talk of change bothers you,” Travis observed.

“It’s not the change,” Chandler said. “It’s how quickly people embrace change without asking what might be lost.”

“Men like your grandfather fear being outpaced. They’ll grab at anything that keeps them ahead.” Travis spat into the corner.

“Even if it costs something important?” Chandler asked.

“That’s how people are.” Travis shrugged. “They only notice what matters when it’s too late and already slipping away.”

The factory bell rang, signaling the end of the final break, and the men returned to work. Chandler shaped another taper, feeling the warmth spread through his palms. The wax formed easily, as it always had. He looked around at the factory, at the men whose hands shaped the light of the city, at the tools used by generations. The world outside might be changing, but inside these walls, the flame still felt steady for now.

The Blisses had brought their tools and secrets to Hanover more than a century earlier, building the company into one of the city’s oldest trades.

Every movement Chandler made echoed something his ancestors had passed forward. Dipping wicks, testing wax, pouring with care, it was all he cared about. To him, candlemaking was more than a family business; it was a glorious inheritance.

Chandler thought about his grandfather's words and other things he had said before. Earl Sr. often said sentiment was a luxury for men with nothing to lose. After a drink or two, he'd call sentiment "childish nonsense." To him, the factory was not a sacred relic but a machine that needed constant oiling and guarding. He could still shape a beautiful candle when he wished, but he rarely did anymore.

These days, Earl Sr.'s thoughts were on profits, contracts, and city politics. Wax no longer soothed him the way it once had. The older he grew, the more he viewed the company not as a legacy but as a burden only he understood how to carry. Where others saw tradition, he saw the risk of falling behind.

The Wick Turns Cold

Outside the factory, the city was awake and noisy. Horses clopped over the cobblestones, men laughed as they spilled out of taverns after a long day of work, and somewhere in the distance a bell from Covenant Cathedral marked the late hour. Hanover wasn't perfect, but it was home. Chandler had joy in knowing his work helped light it.

Broad avenues ran between rows of candle lamps and iron balconies that glimmered softly in the evening haze. By day, merchants filled the streets, their stalls piled high with bread, flowers, and trinkets from the countryside. By night, Hanover glowed with a warm, honey-colored light from a thousand candles in shop windows and church belltowers.

For generations, people had spoken fondly of "the Age of Candlelight," as if it were a beloved ancestor of the city. But lately, Chandler had noticed something strange. Neighbors had begun to describe alleys he knew well like they'd always been dangerous. Stories he'd heard since childhood were being retold in darker tones, portraying candlelight as always being unreliable, one breath away from failure.

It seemed to him the whole city was rewriting its memory, turning candles from symbols of comfort into symbols of inconvenience. Rumors spread of fires that had never happened, of streets left "almost pitch black" on nights he remembered as ordinary. Each story grew more dramatic, as if Hanover wanted something new and was preparing excuses for it before anyone asked.

There were still a few pickpockets and the occasional drunk near the taverns on James Street. Most citizens walked Hanover's streets without fear, trusting their neighbors and the steady glow of candles that had watched over them for generations. The city was proud, busy, and mostly safe, a jewel, lit by human hands.

Earlier in the afternoon, Chandler had gone to dinner with his father, two of his brothers, and a couple of senior candlemakers. As they came out of the restaurant, they saw Earl Bliss Sr. speaking with Mayor Pembroke on the steps of City Hall. Moving with haste to hear the encounter, Earl Jr. hovered half a step behind his father, nodding at everything the mayor said, even when nothing called for agreement. He waved when other business owners passed, trying to match his father's confidence, but his indecisive facial expressions gave him away.

Chandler slowed his pace as they passed. He hadn't meant to stare, but his grandfather's posture caught his attention. Earl Bliss Sr. stood angled slightly away from the mayor, one hand clasped behind his back, the other gesturing only when necessary. When he spoke, it was brief and measured. Chandler couldn't hear the words over the noise of the street, but the mayor leaned into the conversation. Earl Sr. paused before answering questions.

At one point, Earl Sr. scowled and glanced toward City Hall. A faint unease settled in Chandler's chest. He sensed something being discussed had aggravated his grandfather. Earl Sr. smiled respectfully, ending the conversation.

It was a happy coincidence they had run into the mayor that evening or they wouldn't have known. The mayor shared news of a special meeting being held the next day with an announcement they wouldn't want to miss. Earl Sr. had told Chandler's uncle, who then shared it with the rest of the group.

What bothered Chandler wasn't that no one knew what the meeting was about, but everyone spoke as if someone else already did. Chandler's uncle speculated the announcement was a new city project, one requiring a large order of industrial candles. Chandler and a few others rushed back to the factory after dinner. He never worked this late, especially not on a Saturday.

Chandler was certain the Bliss company would secure the contract with the city if they showed the right products. So he did the only thing that made sense, he kept working at the factory. He would trade a night's sleep for a room full of their finest industrial candles if it meant putting them in front of the mayor.

By midnight, the other candlemakers, including his brothers, had gone home. Only Chandler remained, along with an apprentice, Henry Pike, who everyone called, Pike. The boy wasn't yet fifteen years old. He sat on a stool, counting wicks into neat bundles while Chandler worked.

They talked through the hours while they poured and shaped candles. It was now early morning and the conversation had dwindled. By the time the first light crept over the horizon, fifty large industrial candles stood cooling in their crates.

"Master Chandler," Pike asked, breaking the silence, "do you really think Mayor Pembroke will choose us?"

"When he sees the quality we bring him and remembers the Bliss name," Chandler said, hanging another heavy candle to dry, "I don't see why he wouldn't."

A hard knock sounded at the door. Both were slow to react; the long night had worn them down. Pike hurried across the floor and opened it. It was a little after seven in the morning. On a Sunday, the factory would normally have sat dark. A husky man, wearing a messenger's uniform, stepped inside. He had a round face with cold eyes, and he was in a sour mood.

"Mayor Pembroke has sent me," he said. He set a sealed envelope on the counter. "There will be a *demonstration* at City Hall at noon. Candlemakers are required to attend."

Chandler didn't say anything to the courier about his grandfather's conversation with the mayor yesterday. He assumed the letter was an invitation to the meeting. The demeanor of the courier didn't seem like he was in the mood for questions, but Chandler needed to ask one. He hoped to get a competitive advantage with learning more about the project.

"A demonstration of what?" he asked. "And should we bring a few crates of candle samples? We have a full night's work ready for the mayor to see."

The courier hesitated before answering. "No. Just yourselves. Other couriers are already delivering the same message to the rest of your family."

Chandler leaned forward, preparing to ask a follow-up question, but was interrupted before he started to speak.

The courier spoke again, trying to head off any further questions. He continued, "All tradesmen and businesses in Hanover are invited. No one has been asked to bring anything."

He turned to leave, but Pike caught on to what Chandler was doing so he reached out and touched the courier's shoulder. "Please, sir. Can you tell us anything more? What sort of demonstration?"

The courier paused, but his expression shifted, his voice transformed into something like excitement. "A new light has been given to us," he said, tapping the envelope with two fingers. He pulled away, bolting for the door. He shut it with more force than was necessary, sending a sharp gust of wind through the room.

Chandler and Pike froze in place, looking at the stacked crates they'd already moved toward the front. Chandler broke the seal on the envelope. The note inside listed only a time, a place, and one handwritten word: *Mandatory*.

On the front desk, a single candle burned. It was a small tin of wax with a stub for a wick. The draft from the slamming door caught it full on. Instead of bowing and recovering, the flame died outright, leaving a thin thread of smoke winding up into the air. Chandler stared at it. The factory suddenly felt too quiet, as if the breath had gone out of it. The stoves were still warm, the wax still cooling, and yet the room seemed strangely still.

He stepped closer and cupped his hands around the blackened wick, though there was no flame left to protect. They had burned thousands of similar candles in this old, drafty building. A little gust of wind usually made a flame dance. It rarely killed it.

Pike came up beside him, frowning. "That's odd," he said softly. "It wasn't running too low."

"No," Chandler agreed, rubbing the cooled wick between his fingers. "It wasn't."

The boy chewed the inside of his cheek, a habit Chandler had noticed whenever Pike grew nervous. "Do you think it's a sign?"

"A sign of what?" Chandler tried to laugh, but his voice cracked like he was twelve again.

"I don't know," Pike answered. "That something's changing, maybe? That this announcement is not what we thought?"

Chandler didn't reply. He didn't want to make more of it. Still, the thought flooded his mind and refused to leave. He took a match, struck it on the edge of the desk, and held it to the wick. The flame flared, caught for a heartbeat, and then fizzled with a faint hiss. He tried again. The candle refused to light. He frowned, turning his face away so Pike wouldn't see.

"It's just damp," Chandler explained, though he knew it wasn't.

Pike didn't argue. He watched, eyes wide, as if he'd witnessed something he didn't have words for yet. Chandler set the candle aside. He told himself it meant nothing. To pull his thoughts away from it, he walked back to the workbench where some of the industrial candles waited in their crates. The smell of wax, usually pleasant, smelled off. He ran his finger along the rounded sides of the nearest candle. The surfaces were still faintly warm. Each one represented careful hours, pouring, shaping, cooling, and now they looked like a waste of time.

"Should we bring our crates to the demonstration anyway?" Pike asked.

"No," Chandler replied. "If the mayor announces the need for candles, we will run back and get them, but nevertheless, let's prepare for the best." He smiled.

They lifted one of the crates together and carried it closer to the door. Pike struggled with his side but did his best to hide it. Chandler shifted more weight into his own arms without comment. Once they set the crate down, Pike straightened his back and puffed out his chest pretending it had been easy. Chandler chuckled, remembering how he'd behaved at that age.

"Do you think even though the courier told us not to bring our samples..." Pike paused, thinking of what to say. "Do you still think maybe the mayor has something big planned for us? For candlemakers, I mean?"

Chandler let his gaze drift over the rows of finished candles. "He must," he said. "Men don't call meetings like this on a Sunday for nothing. Mayor Pembroke is nothing if not ambitious. The courier said a new light is given to us. That's got to be code for candles, right?"

Pike's face lit up. "Maybe he's planning new street lamps! Or a contract for all the churches and parsonages! You know the pastor always talked about fixing the east wing and the mayor mentioned a full renovation of City Hall last year."

"Maybe," Chandler said, smiling despite himself. "Maybe something better than anything we've thought of."

Truthfully, the idea of new contracts steadied him. It wasn't the money that mattered, his family already did well enough. It was the thought that the city would need more of what they did best, more candles and more light. Something to prove their work still mattered. He wanted to forget the stubborn wick and the way it had left his chest feeling hollow for those few uneasy moments.

Pike went back to his wicks, counting under his breath. "Seventy-seven, seventy-eight, seventy-nine..." He looked up, grinning. "Eighty industrial candles made tonight. We could've done ninety if we'd skipped eating breakfast."

Chandler raised an eyebrow. "You skip meals and your candles will turn out crooked. No one wants a starving candlemaker at the bench."

"Not me," Pike said. "I'll be the first to work with no food and make better candles."

"Impossible," Chandler replied. "If that happened, the whole city would fall apart, and the sun would drop from the sky."

Pike burst into unrestrained laughter, snorting halfway through it. The sound loosened the mood in the room. Chandler picked up another candle and ran his thumb along its smooth length. For a moment, his pride returned. The work looked good.

"You know," he said, still smiling, "I think you might be right."

"Right about what?" Pike blinked.

"About the mayor," Chandler answered. "He talked last year about expanding the night patrols. More patrols mean more lamps. More lamps mean more candles."

Pike's eyes widened. "You really think so?"

"I do," Chandler said. "Candlelight has kept Hanover safe longer than I've been alive. They're not about to throw that away. It was a campaign promise the mayor made last year."

"Yes," Pike said, nodding eagerly. "Yes, that makes sense!"

Chandler set the candle back on the table. "We've done excellent work tonight. We should be proud of it. If the mayor sees these crates, he'll see what this factory can do and of course, the talent of a young apprentice, as well."

Pike stood straighter. "My mother will be thrilled," he said. "She's always saying apprentices don't get noticed for a year or two. Maybe the mayor will mention us. Maybe we'll be in the paper." He caught himself. "Well, maybe *you* will."

Chandler was taken aback by the boy's certainty in him. For all of Chandler's doubts, Pike never shared them. The way the boy looked at him reminded him of how he had once looked at his own father, before responsibility made him dull.

"You worked hard tonight," Chandler said, resting a hand on Pike's shoulder. "I will make sure your mother hears of it."

"I want to do my share," Pike replied, eyes bright.

"You've done more than that," Chandler said, giving his shoulder a gentle pat.

Pike grinned and returned to bundling wicks. Chandler watched him for a moment, struck again by how quickly worry slid off the boy's face. His own negative thoughts weren't so easily shaken. What demonstration invited every business owner, but was mandatory for candlemakers? Why have it on a Sunday, the Lord's Day? And why send a courier to the factory to deliver such a simple message?

Chandler pushed the questions away. He needed rest, not more worrying. But each time he caught sight of the unlit candle on the desk, the tension pinched him. He noticed Pike looked at it again, as well.

"Don't dwell on it," he told Pike, trying to sound offhand. "Candles go out. Nothing more to it."

Pike nodded, but Chandler could tell the boy wasn't convinced even though he wasn't dwelling on it. They finished cleaning the workroom. The familiar sounds of tidying, the scrape of wood, the clink of metal, settled Chandler more than any words could.

Outside, the sun climbed higher. Beautiful light filtered through the upper windows and slid across the crates of finished candles. The sight eased him. Whatever the announcement held, those candles were perfect for the job.

"We should rest," he said. "Today will be a long day."

Pike agreed. "Do you think the mayor will want us to give a speech after we win the contract?"

"I hope not," Chandler said with a faint smile. "Your voice would crack!"

"Yours would crack first, I heard it happen to you earlier," Pike teased.

"Impossible. I'm perfect in every way," Chandler quipped.

The comment earned another laugh from Pike and helped alleviate some of Chandler's anxiety about the announcement. They moved quietly, finishing what little was left to do. Outside, the city carried on, smoke from morning fires rose in thin columns. Family wagons rolled and hooves clunked on stone as people made their way to early morning worship.

Chandler kept glancing at the candle on the desk. The memory of the small flame being snuffed out so easily held on to him in a way he didn't like. He wished the wick would catch light on its own, but that was dreaming. The wick stayed dark. Pike overheard Chandler mumbling, but he ignored it. Pike yawned wide enough to make his eyes water. Chandler chuckled.

"Go home, my young friend," he said. "Get some sleep. You've earned it."

"You'll sleep, too?" Pike asked.

"Yes," Chandler answered, though he wasn't sure it was true. "We'll meet at City Hall five minutes before noon."

They walked toward the front of the factory. As they passed the receptionist's desk, Chandler paused. He reached out and adjusted the candle that refused to burn, setting it upright in the center of the desk as if it were keeping watch.

"Interesting morning," Pike suggested.

"Yes," Chandler agreed with a smile. "And the rest of the day will be even more interesting!"

They stepped out into the morning light. Chandler turned back once more, letting his eyes rest on the cold, lifeless wick. He shut the door behind them and made his way home.

The Demonstration

Noon was nearing and City Hall looked more presentable than usual. The grime had been scrubbed from its stone face, the fountains shined, the pigeons driven off, and the front steps were washed clean. It was a sizable government building with a front courtyard designed to impress.

On this Sunday, most of the shops were closed. A wooden podium stood at the top of the stairs of City Hall, and banners with golden tassels hung along the railings, announcing a celebration or holiday no one could name.

The banners displayed an eye with a torch at its center, a strange emblem. Chandler studied it for a few seconds, the moment stretching in a way he couldn't quite grasp. The banner's material was expensive, high-gloss, and unnaturally well made.

Business owners and their workers crowded in front of City Hall. A barricade kept them from going up the stairs, so naturally, they pressed as close to the barrier as possible. Chandler had never seen so many trades gathered in one place. There were barbers, plumbers, blacksmiths, grocers, and dozens more.

A few hundred feet away, Chandler spotted several of his kin, Earl Bliss Sr. and Earl Jr. among them. His brothers were trading polite words and making small talk. Everyone wore their Sunday best, as they had come from morning services.

Earl Sr. stood with one hand clenched behind his back; his posture was straight and alert. He wasn't staring at the banners because he was studying the mayor, the size of the crowd, and listening to the banter of those around him. Whenever Pembroke or a council member glanced his way, Earl Sr. straightened his posture more, like a man ready to seize an opening. Chandler recognized the glint in his grandfather's eyes. It was the same look he wore whenever there was talk of expansion.

"Stay close to me, Pike," Chandler encouraged his apprentice.

Pike, shorter than most of the men around him, craned his neck to see. He wore his best button-down shirt and a jacket that had clearly been someone else's first. His trousers rode up high above his ankles like high waters. Like most in their trade, he didn't come from money.

"I had no idea there were so many trades," Pike whispered. "Look, there are bakers, tailors, and shoe shiners!"

"And all of us dragged out on a Sunday at the same hour," Chandler snickered, lifting an eyebrow. "Whatever this is, the mayor must consider it important. Perhaps he's raising taxes again." He rolled his eyes and made a goofy face, joking.

"That's not funny, Master Chandler," Pike fretted. He could barely afford bread and milk as it was.

"You're right," Chandler apologized. "Tax increases are never funny."

The volume of the crowd was incredible, with everyone trying to speak over one another. Without anyone directing it, workers sorted themselves into clusters, trades flocking together like geese. Chimney sweeps were the easiest to spot, their faces and hands stained permanently with soot. The general mood was curious, even good-humored, kept in check only by anxious waiting.

Mayor Pembroke, who had been chatting with the bankers and investors, finished his small talk. He turned and began climbing the steps toward the podium. Two chairs were carried out and set a few feet away. A man Chandler couldn't see well took one of the chairs behind the podium. He didn't recognize him, but Chandler was having déjà vu, as if he had seen him somewhere before. The man was smiling from ear to ear. The other chair remained empty. It was clearly reserved for someone important.

A small commotion stirred behind the podium, close to the entry of City Hall and off to the left. First, a crew of twenty men assembled what appeared to be a huge tent. Mayor Pembroke stepped aside, making space for the uniformed men to move around. Their jackets were stiff and new, each marked with the same eye-and-torch. They moved more like choreographed performers than laborers.

All sides of the tent were draped with dark velvet curtains. Next, several men in dress uniforms walked behind a shroud. They were carrying something long and slender with copper wires dangling from it. They worked like stagehands at a magic show, feeding the object into the back of the tent. Long wires coming from under the tent were joined to a thicker cord and anchored to the ground.

The crowd pressed in as their boots scraped together. Apprentices everywhere rose up on their toes for a better look. Every craft in Hanover stood shoulder to shoulder. Trades that normally paid each other little attention were packed together like cousins at an overcrowded Thanksgiving table. Chandler picked out familiar faces, a tinsmith who bought church candles, and the old woodcarver from the market.

In the restless swell of bodies pressed together, Chandler's attention snagged on one face he didn't recognize. She wasn't calling out or craning for a better view, yet her presence drew his gaze. She had a genuine smile and a quiet confidence. A few loose strands of hair framed her face, giving her an effortless grace. She was plainly beautiful, not polished or fake. He didn't know her name, but in that moment, Chandler wished he did.

Pike tugged on his sleeve pulling back his attention. "What do you think it is?" he whispered, eyes fixed on the tent.

Chandler had no answer. Every instinct told him this was not some harmless carnival tent. The city did not summon every guild, shop owner, and apprentice on a Sunday for a simple show. Yet the tent stood tall and silent. It was too delicate and too quiet to seem dangerous. It didn't roar like a furnace or hiss like a steam engine.

On the far side of the square, Earl Bliss Sr. and Earl Jr. leaned forward as if drawn by a magnet, their faces bright with anticipation. Chandler's stomach turned at the sight. His grandfather's hands were locked behind his back. Chandler couldn't get a read on their thoughts based on their facial expressions. Were they excited or afraid?

Pembroke watched from the podium until the men finished. A city clerk stepped up to the podium and snapped his fingers. Two uniformed men took hold of the front corner of the velvet curtains. The curtain across the front of the tent was pulled away as the men yanked it forcefully. The men stepped inside the curtain flanking each side of the lamppost like guards.

The curtain dropped with a heavy swoosh, and Chandler felt the universe narrow into a tunnel. The crowd swayed forward in one slow and collective movement. Chandler stayed rooted and didn't budge an inch. Something tightened at the back of his neck and his knees felt weak. His breath became heavy.

Behind the curtain, in the middle of the tent, stood a unique street lamp. It was a metal post topped by an odd glass bubble. The other three sides of the curtain remained drawn, casting the lamp in a pocket of shadow.

At first glance, the lamppost itself looked normal enough. It was clearly a newer design, but still like what was already on every street corner. It had a metal shaft and a rounded base. But the thing on top of it, the glass bulb, drew his attention and refused to let go. It was smooth like river stone and utterly seamless. Candle jars always had tiny bubbles, ripples, and flaws that caught the light. Lantern glass had its subtle waves. This bulb had none.

For a moment, Chandler felt hopeful. Street lamps meant candles, and candles meant business. He regretted listening to the courier and leaving behind the samples he and Pike had made the night before. In his head, he calculated how fast he could run back to the factory and grab a few samples.

Pike tugged on Chandler's sleeve. "Is that the new light the courier mentioned?"

"If it is," Chandler joked, "it looks a lot like the old light." He let out a laugh louder than he should have.

The crowd was quiet, but there were still a few sidebar conversations. The strange man in the chair tilted his head and smiled at Chandler, as if he'd heard his comment. Chandler wasn't sure what to make of him staring. The lamppost looked ordinary enough, aside from the wires and the odd glass "candle" sitting on top.

When Mayor Pembroke declared to the crowd, "**The future of light is here**," Chandler's pulse spiked. He didn't understand why the comment unnerved him so deeply.

For a heartbeat, nothing happened, but then, with a flick of a blue lever, the "candle" inside the glass ignited with a burst of light. It didn't look like a flame as there was no rise or flicker. There was no wick, no match, no oil, and no wax, just a burst of light, bright as the sun, sealed inside the domed glass.

Chandler's stomach gurgled with nausea. He suddenly felt disoriented, as though the ground had shifted under his feet. He brought a hand briefly to his mouth, breathing slowly through his nose.

The light filled the tent, but it bore no resemblance to a candle. Candlelight did not fill corners or cast hard shadows. Candles forgave imperfections and softened edges. A man near the front of the crowd rubbed his forehead. Another squinted like he was staring into the sun. There was a dull tightness behind Chandler's eyes as he investigated the light. The light didn't move or respond.

The crowd did not speak, gasp, or cheer. Hundreds of people stood perfectly still, as if frozen in time. Even the restless shifting of bodies had ceased. Chandler's heartbeat echoed in his ears.

The light was terrible in its perfection, yet undeniably beautiful. It revealed everything. Dandruff dusted the shoulders of the uniformed men. Deep lines marked their faces. The tools hanging from their belts were covered in scratches. Nothing could hide from the light. There was no warmth to it, just an unimaginable power on display.

Chandler's mind fell into a vision of Hanover transformed. The vision only lasted a couple of seconds as the future passed before him. Every factory, home, and shop in town was suffocated in bright light. No more candle flickers, lamplighters tending wicks, and a world evolved beyond a need for flames. The vision left him as quickly as it came.

The silence of the crowd stretched too long! It was as if the city of Hanover itself was holding its breath. Someone mumbled, "My God," and the sound of the crowd rushed back in a collective burst of tremendous noise, not praise, just noise. Chandler exhaled, realizing it was he who had been holding his breath. Pike clutched onto his sleeve with a firm grip.

"Do you see that?" Pike screeched, his voice trembling like he was witnessing a miracle.

Chandler nodded in agreement, though his gaze remained fixed on the bulb. He felt unsteady, as if he had witnessed something unnatural. The light went off, then on again, then off, then on, then off, then on. The stutter of the light happened in the blink of an eye, so quickly Chandler wondered if it was all in his head. The man sitting behind the podium had stopped smiling until the light became constant again.

Once again, like a tsunami's wave, a unified gasp rippled through the crowd, followed by silence. Chandler took a half step forward, drawn closer by fascination. The bulb held his gaze the way a storm on the horizon holds a sailor's. The light was stunning, terrible, and impossible to ignore.

Even the pigeons that had crept back to the rooftops were still, as if they, too, understood something was different about the light. Chandler felt it in his chest. It was like feeling the air change before a storm breaks. The crowd waited.

A single bell rang from Covenant Cathedral. Noon had passed an hour ago, but it felt like only minutes. Mayor Pembroke, recognizing the crowd was uncertain, quickly introduced the man from the chair as "Sullivan," and the man rose to his feet. He wore polished shoes, a long, dark coat, and a top hat. The eye-and-torch emblem gleamed on a silver pin on his lapel. He had a confident, clean smile that felt practiced but not stiff, and his face had distinct features making him look alert and self-assured. The way he stood and carried himself suggested he was comfortable in the spotlight, like someone used to being in front of large crowds.

Chandler finally recognized him as he had seen his picture a few times in the Hanover newspaper. He was Sullivan Vale, Director of Hanover Industrial Development. He was an engineer brought in from New York after Pembroke won his last election.

"Citizens of Hanover," Vale called, his voice carrying. "Skilled men. Tradeswomen. Artisans. Blacksmiths. People of talent. You are the keepers of our noble crafts. Thank you for coming on this beautiful Sunday."

Chandler watched him closely. Vale's hands were spotless, no calluses, no ink stains, and no trace of labor. He was a city man through and through.

"We gather today," Vale continued, pausing theatrically, "on the edge of a new dawn for our immaculate Hanover."

Whispers stirred across the crowd. Hanover had heard many speeches like this before, typically right before taxes went up or rations tightened. Chandler sensed the cynicism in the crowd, as it was palpable. No one knew what Vale was driving at with his remarks, but they were eager to find out.

"For millennia," Vale proclaimed, "humanity has depended on a flame," he paused dramatically, "a flame to cook, to heat, to light our streets and push back the darkness."

Chandler's spirits lifted. At least Vale understood the significance of candlemakers. He considered running back to fetch the samples they'd made. He was eager to show that the Bliss Candle Factory was forward thinking and ready for whatever upgrade the city planned. He'd never seen a sealed-glass lamp like this nor one lit with a switch, but he was sure he could learn how to make it.

Vale's tone shifted. "Flame is beautiful. It is warm. It lives in our hearts as the foundation of our city's origins." His eyes swept the candlemakers, lingering pointedly on Earl Bliss Sr. "But unfortunately, flame is also drab. It is archaic. It is old-fashioned and imperfect."

Chandler's jaw tightened as tears formed at the corners of his eyes. His father and grandfather nodded along as though every word Vale said made perfect sense. Mayor Pembroke kept looking to the bankers, investors, and business owners for approval.

"Flame is dangerous," Vale pressed on. "It devours without hesitation, fills our lungs with smoke, burns homes, kills families. It demands sacrifice, fuel, wax, tallow, labor, and time," He gave a pompous laugh. "And of course... it is literally burning our money."

A few uneasy chuckles drifted through the crowd, including some candlemakers, not out of humor, but uncertainty.

"Progress," Vale continued passionately, "does not come to those who wait. If flame costs us so dearly, must we remain bound to it forever? Hold that thought." He held up his hand.

Director Vale motioned to the men in uniforms to remove the barricades. He turned and walked into City Hall. At the direction of Mayor Pembroke, the crowd followed, shuffling up the stairs until everyone had arrived. Inside, the windows were covered, and the great hall was pitch dark. When the heavy doors shut, a wave of confusion rippled through the room.

"We will not be prisoners to a flame any longer!" Vale stood on the clerk's desk as his voice rang out.

He pressed a button and the room erupted in light. Bulbs had been mounted on metal arms that flared with a light no one had ever experienced. The lights didn't flicker; they stood still like a soldier on guard. They were a hard white glow that cut across the hall like a blade. Chandler's heart tumbled within his chest as Pike clung to his sleeve.

"Behold, good citizens of Hanover," Vale roared, "I present to you... Artificial Illumination!"

The crowd gasped; they were in a state of shock. The city workers in uniform applauded, loudly clapping their hands together. Chandler squinted, his eyes strained from the brightness in the room. The light didn't dance, it didn't move, it didn't smoke, it simply stared back at him. Standing next to Chandler, Pike mouthed something that might have been important, but Chandler barely heard it over the heavy beating of his own heart.

The lights in City Hall made a slight humming sound. They didn't crackle or hiss. They didn't glow or flicker. They simply sat there. Chandler tried to swallow, but his throat was dry, as if he was chewing on sawdust. He thought about reaching up and laying his palm against the glass to see if it was warm or as cold as ice. Did it produce heat at all? The questions shot through his head faster than he could think about them. He didn't know what to do. He was afraid, yet still wanted to know more about the flameless lamps.

The desire to know more and fear pulled at him in opposite directions. He felt like a flame caught between a steady burn and a sudden gust of wind. A memory flashed through his mind of himself as a boy at a workbench in the factory when he had cupped his hands around a candle his father had made. The flame felt alive, it was warm, and it had responded to the movement of his hands.

These lamps produced dead light. Again, Chandler saw all of Hanover lit by lamps like this. The vision haunted him, springing into his mind without his consent. The soft light of candles would be replaced with these unblinking eyes watching from doorways and street corners. He pictured these bulbs mounted over every shop, hanging in every home, humming faintly like soulless machines. A shiver ran down his back and into his feet.

Dead Light

"Vale has captured the sun in a glass bottle!" a banker shouted.

"It's a miracle! An act of God!" an investor bellowed.

"Marvelous! Stupendous! Magnificent!" a few well-dressed businessmen declared at the top of their lungs.

"Isn't it a thing of beauty?" Earl Bliss Sr.'s voice boomed from the crowd.

Chandler moved across the crowd, attempting to get closer to his family, who were now standing with Mayor Pembroke nearby. All the wealthy men had formed a group. He shouldered, elbowed, and shoved his way until he got within a few feet. All the while, the crowd was erupting with incoherent noise.

"Grandpa," Chandler yelled, desperate to get his attention. "Grandpa, can you believe they're doing this to us?"

"Doing what to us? They are doing this for us, for all of Hanover," Earl Sr. reprimanded Chandler.

Vale approached, jumping down from the clerk's desk and dashing through the crowd. Chandler's tongue felt thick, like he had chewed on taffy. Earl Jr., his father, appeared baffled by Chandler's comment.

"Is something wrong?" Mayor Pembroke asked. "You seem troubled, son."

"I'm concerned about what this means for our family's company," Chandler admitted.

Director Vale cut in smoothly. "Imagine the candles you could make with Artificial Illumination! Night shifts without fear, fewer mistakes, and happier workers." He moved away before Chandler could respond. He climbed atop another clerk's desk, addressing the crowd once more in a booming voice.

"This single bulb burns for two thousand hours without needing fuel. It cannot be blown out by wind. It cannot burn down your home. It will make Hanover the safest city on earth," declared Vale as he paused dramatically. "We may call it Artificial Illumination, but you may refer to it as the promise of a better tomorrow."

A chill crawled up Chandler's spine, and he didn't know what to say, so he didn't say anything.

Pike hesitated, then bravely raised his hand. "Director Vale... what about our candles? Our lamps? Sir, our daily bread depends on them."

Chandler detected the weight of the room shift toward the boy. Every instinct told him to stand beside Pike and add his voice. Chandler asking would give the question far more weight than a trembling teenager. He opened his mouth, then stopped. He thought of his grandfather and his father nodding along with the investors. Pembroke was already watching people closely to see how they reacted.

Speaking up with Pike would not change the answer, he told himself. It would only mark him as a detractor. Surely, there would be a better, more tactful opportunity to voice his concerns; a time when emotions were cooler and consequences less immediate. Chandler stayed quiet, keeping his hands at his sides. He let Pike's question hang in the air.

Vale turned to Pike with a practiced, sympathetic smile. "Candles have brought us far and you have my respect. You'll be pleased to know we have already discussed these concerns with Earl Bliss Sr., and he is eager to use Artificial Illumination. He foresees new prosperity for candlemakers."

The investors, bankers, and business owners started chanting, "Artificial Illumination, Artificial Illumination, Artificial Illumination!" The rhythm of the chant was off-key and clunky. Chandler's father began clapping and chanting along. Chandler's fists clenched, his fingernails digging into his palms.

Vale, noticing how terrible the chanting sounded, put his hands up to silence them. Appearance mattered more to him than anything. It was then, once they stopped, a city worker, in the back, dressed in a janitor's uniform, began chanting, slowly, "AI, AI, AI." It was soft and unsure at first, but then near the front of the room, another city worker, wearing laborer's clothes, joined in with the same chant.

It was unclear whether the city workers were plants or not. Vale waited, reading the crowd's reaction, and they loved it. Vale started chanting along like they had rehearsed this before the demonstration. Pembroke pushed the white-collar crowd to start in, as well, followed by the business owners encouraging their workers to chant. Some joined in, but most did not.

The chanting, hooting, and hollering continued for several minutes. Saying AI was easier for the crowd to recite and it sounded pleasant to the ear. Vale waited until the crowd took a natural pause from their chanting.

"I know, my friends," Vale's eyes scanned the room and landed on Chandler, "change is difficult, but it is inevitable. Embrace AI, and I promise no industry will suffer. This is not your enemy; it is a gift to all."

Around him, the white-collar crowd roared and cheered louder. They hailed "AI" as though it were a thing they'd known for years, since their birth. Some business owners grumbled, not in fear, but in worry about not getting AI fast enough.

Chandler stood in the middle of it all, silent. A new light had been given, but for him, a deeper darkness had arrived. He didn't know whether to cheer, cry, or run screaming out of City Hall. This new thing, may it be called Artificial Illumination or AI, hadn't done anything to him, yet. It simply existed, and it already commanded Hanover. Being a candlemaker was his life and, for the first time, he realized how fragile it was, like a sandcastle sitting too close to the rising tide.

The crowd's chatter and applause eventually came to a halt. Chandler perceived a ripple of uneasiness passing through the workers. He realized he wasn't alone, although he was not sure if anyone else understood why they felt uneasy in their spirit. The investors, bankers, and business owners remained in their own group as they exchanged pats on the back.

Chandler deliberately moved away from them. To his left, the bakers, who worked seven days a week, were still dusted faintly in flour from their morning batches. They traded puzzled looks with each other. A baker's apprentice named Jeffrey, a good man, from Conrad & Sons Bakery, scratched his chin with his pointer finger.

"Looks fancy," Jeffrey muttered, squinting at a bulb. "But how in the blue blazes do you light it? It's got no wick, no oil bowl, it's all wrong."

"Maybe it gives off enough heat to rise dough faster and make our lives easier?" another baker optimistically responded.

"A lamp shouldn't be used to bake with!" Jeffrey grunted.

A few steps behind them, two tailors stood with measuring tapes looped around their necks. They intently studied the lights.

"I don't trust it," said one of the tailors named Kimberly. "Look at the reflection it puts out! It's too bright and overpowering! Come on, light that doesn't flicker is not natural."

Her younger sister, Gloria, looked down at her hand, still bandaged from a needle slip. "If it brightens up the shop, then I might thread a needle without accidentally poking my own eye out," she joked.

"Light changes everything, sister," Kimberly laughed and patted Gloria on the back. "Cloth looks different in the flame of a lamp or candle. If this thing shifts our colors even a hair, I swear on my shears, I'll march back into this place and have words with Mayor Pembroke."

Near them, the cobblers had gathered in a tight group of about five workers. The shoemakers, Valerie and John, wore identical leather aprons. Valerie was smiling and John had crossed his arms, clearly not impressed with the AI lamps.

"Those fake bulbs won't do a thing for our work," John snorted. "Shoes don't care what lights we use in the shop. We don't need those; we will keep our candles and lamps!"

"Maybe," Valerie replied, "but a brighter bench means fewer missed stitches. Let's not forget there will be no more candle wax dripping on good leather."

John playfully elbowed her. "You're missing the point. If those fake lamps replace our candles, who knows what's next. If we don't resist this new stuff, one day they'll want machines cutting leather instead of our hands."

"Machines?" Valerie smirked, laughing at him. "Now you're being dramatic."

On the far edge of the crowd, the blacksmiths stood together. They were rugged men who lived and worked by the heat of fire. They were broad-chested, covered in ash and soot. They stared at the AI lamps like deer eyeballing a wolf pack.

Big George, who was not a man to be trifled with, rubbed a hand over his bald head. "If that thing's metal and wire, someone forged the parts."

"Aye, but once they've built a way to make the same parts repeatedly, they don't need us shaping them. Some fancy new press will stamp them out by the dozen," another blacksmith grunted.

"Machines make soft men. A world run by metal and glass is no world I want for my sons. AI lamps... this is garbage." George spat on the clean City Hall tile floor.

Behind them, a gaggle of about ten seamstresses whispered among each other. They fanned themselves while chitchatting.

"Looks heavenly, doesn't it?" one of the seamstresses admired.

"Looks frightening if you ask me," scoffed another.

"It looks like stars fell from the sky. It's like Hanover City Hall is a place for royalty," a third added her opinion.

"Maybe, this is the blessing we all prayed for?" the first seamstress chimed in, again.

"Or the curse we prayed against!" shrieked the other.

Near Chandler, the butchers barked at each other. These were men who carried the faint smell of smoke and meat even on holy days. They stared at the AI lamps with a different sort of calculation. One tipped his cap and let out a low whistle.

"Those would sure brighten the meat displays," he asserted. "Customers could see cuts clear as day. We could charge more for premium cuts when they see the high quality."

"They might see too much. No good for us if every blemish shows. We may have to charge less when they see the flaws," the other butcher frowned.

As the butchers continued their argument, Chandler noticed the beautiful woman among them, the same woman that had caught his eye outside. One of the butchers, presumably her father, said her name, "Rae." She glanced at Chandler, her smile lingered on him a heartbeat longer than courtesy required, sending an unexpected rush of heat through his chest.

Chandler composed himself and looked towards the farmers, who had been summoned in from the countryside by courier and stood in a group. Their faces were browned by the sun, and their hair was wild from the wind. They smelled like their work, that of earth and animals. They were not men of many words, and they were hesitant to speak up, but they, too, opined.

"If that light could be mounted on the barns," a young farmhand suggested, "we wouldn't lose so many hens to foxes. This AI stuff would greatly help us."

An older farmer shook his head. "Foxes will fear it for a couple nights at best until they get used to it. It's not a long-term solution; that's for sure."

From the back, nearest the City Hall entrance, the chimney sweeps stood in a cluster. They wore smudged gray slacks even though they were in their cleanest clothes. Their silence spoke for itself, but eventually they, too, spoke their minds. It didn't help that the owner of the chimney sweep company was laughing it up across the room with Mayor Pembroke and Director Vale.

"These AI lamps are going to put us out of work," one chimney sweep cried.

"I've cleaned chimneys and tended candles for six decades. Fire keeps men warm, lights their house, and the smoke pays my wages. If these things burn no fuel..." An old chimney sweep bowed his head, "we'll be homeless on the streets in our own city before long."

The crowd's volume swelled within City Hall. It was like a strong wind was driving in dry leaves. People were fearful, hopeful, envious, wondering, and in disbelief all at the same time. Every trade saw AI through its own eyes, some in awe, some in panic. Every trade worker saw its future bending in a unique way.

Chandler did not speak; he only listened. For every hopeful voice, another sounded afraid. For every amazed person, another was grieving something they couldn't yet name. He stood motionless as the noise of the hall pressed in around him. Around him, voices rose and overlapped, but Chandler did not join them.

He stood there frozen, caught between dread and wonder. It was a battle between the world that had shaped him and the one that was arriving whether he welcomed it or not. His mind screamed at him to look away, to ignore it, to preserve the only way of life he had ever known. His heart insisted he continue watching the moment history changed. He hated being afraid of AI and hated, equally, being impressed by it.

Effective Immediately

People poured out of City Hall. Chandler and Pike followed. The Covenant Cathedral tower bell rang out four times. At Earl Sr.'s instruction, all employees were to head back to the factory to discuss the coming week's productivity plans. It was an odd request, but no one questioned it. They crossed Alexander Bridge in silence. The bridge arched high over the sluggish river. Chandler brushed the iron railing with his fingertips as they walked.

The water below looked like dull metal, and it reflected the glimmers of afternoon light. Brick rooftops, market stalls, and distant church towers framed the horizon. The hand-blown lanterns lined the bridge waiting patiently for dusk when their flames would paint the river gold again. Chandler questioned how long that tradition would last.

A soft breeze carried unique scents through Hanover. They smelled of fresh bread and hay bales, and someone nearby was baking apple pies. Usually, this would have comforted him, but not today. He glanced again at the iron lampposts donning candles on top and was faced with a reminder of something slipping away.

"Why are you so upset? Your grandfather supports AI, and he's an honorable man. Plus, Director Vale is trustworthy. So... why?" Pike finally spoke.

There was no sarcasm in Pike's voice, only honest confusion. Chandler stared down at the river, then at the candles lining the bridge rails. In a few hours, each would glow with a candle's warm pulse. Someday soon, they wouldn't.

"There'll always be people who prefer the old light," Chandler said quietly. "For rituals and for reading. For softness and comfort. Not everyone will want AI... right?" he asked.

"Do you not trust your own grandfather or father? Director Vale seems like a great guy!" Pike's brow furrowed.

"No!" The word escaped Chandler's mouth like vomit. He threw up his hands. "No, Pike! No, I don't trust this AI stuff!"

Silence lingered between Pike's question and Chandler's statement. His cheeks had become red in color. Pike was trying to figure out how to approach his friend and mentor. He had no intention of further agitating Chandler, but he felt he was acting unreasonable.

"It was incredible, though!" Pike exclaimed. "The power of the sun with a switch. We could work faster. Make more candles. It would mean fewer mistakes, more profit, and less crime. Let's not forget about improved safety."

Pike sounded like he was repeating Vale's speech, but Chandler was not mad at him. Chandler closed his eyes and muttered to himself, "Fire is beautiful, too!"

"Yeah, until it burns your house down!" Pike replied with scorn while still trying to sound respectful.

There was no more talking, although Pike tried to rally the conversation to something more pleasant, like going out later to purchase an apple pie. Back at the factory, Chandler did what he always did. He grabbed a candle and lit it. This was more out of habit than anything. The flame sputtered, then steadied. It released a sweet lavender scent. The candle soothed him. The glow softened the cluttered shelves, the tubs of wax, and the rows of tools. This was his world and he cherished being back even though it was Sunday.

On the counter lay the courier's envelope. Chandler stared at it, then touched it to the candle flame. It curled, turned red, blackened, and burned like it was soaked in kerosene. Strangely, watching it burn made him feel better. The door opened. Earl Sr., Earl Jr., two of Chandler's brothers, and Director Vale entered, laughing about dinner plans.

"Ah, Chandler," Vale said, placing a hand on his shoulder. "Your grandfather speaks highly of you. He told me you'll lead this factory one day. Oh, how I admire the ambition of the youth. Perhaps I'll recruit you into the Department of Industrial Development before he hands you the keys to the factory," he joked, then winked at Chandler's grandfather.

Chandler smiled politely and tried to downplay the compliment. Pike beamed. He'd always admired Chandler's talent and leadership skills. The expression on the brothers' faces suggested they were less than pleased hearing their younger sibling receive such a compliment. The only angrier scowl in the room was from Chandler's own father. Vale seemed pleasant enough, yet was too slick for Chandler's taste. Maybe asking questions would be wiser than assuming the worst.

Before Chandler could speak, Vale pulled out pieces of folded parchment from his coat and handed one to everyone, including Chandler, which was a copy of the same letter. Vale read from his own:

Dear Respected Candlemakers of Hanover,

This memorandum is effective immediately. As *the city transitions to Artificial Illumination* (AI), *the production of candles, lantern wicks, and all fire-*

based goods is to be reduced by seventy percent over the next three months.

All public-candle contracts are suspended or converted to transitional agreements. The Department of Industrial Development will provide full compensation during this period. Details of reimbursement will be provided within five calendar days.

Please be advised: Unauthorized production of candles or sales beyond approved quotas will result in fines and judicial penalty. Together, we will build a brighter future with AI.

Thank you,

Sullivan Vale

Director of Industrial Development

Chandler read the memorandum twice, unable to understand how his grandfather had agreed to this. Pike nodded along, whispering, "It makes sense," under his breath.

"Grandpa," Chandler said, trying to reason with him, "if every home and shop uses AI, they won't need candles anymore."

"That's small thinking," Earl Sr. scolded. "AI will elevate us. AI will expand our horizons. Plus, we'll be compensated during the transition. It's a terrific opportunity and we are thankful for Director Vale's vision of the future."

"AI will streamline everything," Earl Jr. jumped into the conversation. "We will have faster production with fewer errors. Think about it! Pike could rise in the company with us doubling our output. Imagine the raises we could give. Maybe Pike here could get pants that actually fit him."

"You know what?" Vale leaned towards Earl Jr., "I've heard rumors of a major candle company in Louisville that wants to relocate here. They're eager for AI. It would be a shame if the Bliss Candle Factory lost its position in Hanover because a certain son wouldn't support progress."

Earl Sr. and Jr.'s tempers flared, turning their frustration on Chandler. Pike looked uneasy and Chandler felt cornered. His concerns for the company and for his families' future had been taken as disloyalty. Chandler swallowed hard as the sawdust in his mouth had returned with a vengeance.

"I will embrace Artificial Illumination," he said in desperation. "Maybe I'm wrong about it. Maybe it's good."

"That's the spirit," Vale said with a nod. "AI is going to change your life forever; you wait."

Vale folded the memorandum once more, smoothing the crease with his thumb. He locked eyes with Chandler, like a poker player trying to read him. Chandler stood tall and confident. Vale's lips pulled tight as he examined how Chandler would respond to the uncomfortable silence. Chandler did not break under pressure and kept a fierce gaze.

"This will be an adjustment," Vale spoke, coughing. "But people adapt faster than they think."

Chandler nodded politely, though something in his heart felt hollow. Vale was trying to sell him the value of AI, but if AI were valuable, wouldn't it sell itself? He recalled the deadness of the artificial lamp humming in City Hall. It had not flickered or acknowledged their presence when they moved.

"Director Vale," Chandler was careful to not raise his voice.

"Yes?" Vale looked up, already half-turned toward the door.

Chandler had more questions to ask. In his head, he pondered the best way to sound thoughtful rather than defiant. This was the only opportunity he would have to ask them before tomorrow when the reduction order would be implemented in the factory.

"What happens," he asked, "if someone *chooses* not to use AI?"

The question landed with Vale, and he did not answer at first. His cheesy smile held, but the corners of his mouth were tight. The question caught him off guard, like he had not anticipated anyone being so bold to ask it.

"They won't," Vale responded.

Chandler tilted his head, again making direct eye contact with Vale, whose smile was interrupted for only a moment to answer the question.

"When a thing is safer, cleaner, and superior in every measurable way, choice becomes irrelevant." Vale added.

He gave Chandler, and Earl Sr., a polite gesture, as if the matter was settled by simple arithmetic. There was a pompous, yet unique soothing to his words. There was venom dripping from his teeth, yet there was also a sincere gentleness in how he responded.

"People will follow beautiful light," Vale nodded at Earl Sr. "They always have."

Vale turned and left the factory. His footsteps were brisk and confident against the factory floor. Even the way he opened the door was eloquent and polished. The members of the Bliss family and most of the candlemakers dispersed as a group. They were eager to finish their Sunday at home with their families. The candle Chandler had lit continued to glow.

The only ones remaining were Chandler, Pike, and a dozen candlemakers, including a few apprentices. For a long moment, no one moved at all. The air felt unsettled, like the walls themselves were unsure what to do next. There was no work that needed to be done. They stood there, looking at each other.

"Well," Travis said, folding his arms, "I suppose that's progress?" He had broken the silence with a humorless laugh.

No one answered him. A few men exchanged looks; they were all thinking the same thing. Others stared at their hands, suddenly conscious of every burn scar and callus. One apprentice reached instinctively for a wick cutter, then stopped, as there was no candle to work on.

"What exactly does *reduce by seventy percent* mean?" Samuel Roy asked. "Seventy percent of what?"

"Seventy percent of *us*," Travis spat.

"That's not what they said," Pike was the only one that protested. "They said we'd be compensated."

"Yea, and how long does that last?" Travis replied sarcastically.

Pike glanced at Travis, who had been popping his knuckles like he was preparing for a fist fight. A ripple of sidebar conversations happened among them. Samuel started talking about *permits*, *inspections*, and *quotas*. A few of the candlemakers began doing rough calculations of the reduction orders. Apprentices, trying to act like the older men, whispered to one another.

Earl Bliss Sr., who had walked out minutes before, came back into the factory unnoticed. He cleared his throat, and the sound of his grumbling voice alone pulled the room to an uncomfortable silence again.

"There will be no speculation," he commanded the room. "Do you all understand me?"

"Yes, yes sir," they responded with one voice.

"Speculation breeds panic," declared Earl Sr. "We have been given clear direction, and by God, we will follow it without resistance."

Travis opened his mouth, then closed it again, his jaw clenched. He fought back the words he so desperately wanted to speak.

"This factory has survived wars, shortages, and fire," Earl Sr. continued. "It will survive this, as well. Tomorrow, you will return to your stations and follow the mandate to a T."

The words *your stations* rang hollow in Chandler's ears. Earl Sr. instructed the men, except for Chandler and Pike, to leave the factory and return home. Earl Sr. briefly walked to his office, for what purpose they didn't know. Pike stood beside Chandler, his eyes bright with anticipation. He was caught between joyful enthusiasm and anxious fear.

"Did you hear him?" Pike whispered. "Director Vale, I mean. Two thousand hours, Master Chandler. Without fuel. That's... that's remarkable!"

Chandler did not respond as he watched in anticipation for his grandfather to return.

“And think about it,” Pike went on. “If we don’t have to worry about drafts or smoke, we could work faster and safer with fewer mistakes.” His voice lifted with intense excitement. “We could have night shifts to double our production, and we will all get raises!” He looked down at his high-water pants.

Chandler, hearing the passion in Pike’s voice, looked at the boy, whose optimism was earnest. It came from a place Chandler recognized painfully well, the place that still believed effort was everything. Chandler had learned life was not a meritocracy as he once, too, had thought. Life was men clawing past each other through politics and scandal.

“Yes,” Chandler said. “Politicians promise a lot in their speeches.”

“You don’t sound convinced.” Pike crossed his arms.

“I’m thinking,” Chandler replied.

“That’s good. My mother always says thinking is how you get ahead in life,” Pike uncrossed his arms, relieved.

Chandler managed a faint smile, but something inside his soul dreaded hearing the advice of Pike’s mother. The philosophy she had taught Pike was rooted in fallacy. Get ahead of what? Get ahead of whom? He did not agree with the premise, but he was not about to insult or make an argument against the boy's mom.

"Master Chandler?" Pike added, quieter now. "Vale promised no one would suffer and I believe he means it."

Chandler didn't reply right away. His gaze drifted across the factory floor, to the racks of tapers, to the tools that had passed through generations of hands. He imagined inspectors counting and measuring them before deciding how many candles could be made that day. How long until they were told to cease *all* production?

"Men like Vale say many things," Chandler finally responded.

Before Pike could respond, Earl Bliss Sr.'s voice cut through the space behind them.

"Chandler, come walk with me," he held out his arm.

Pike pretended not to listen at first, and the further they moved toward the end of the hall, the less he could hear. Chandler could feel the tips of his toes striking the inside edge of his shoes. Earl Sr. stopped near the tall windows overlooking the street. The late afternoon light filtered in as the candles were being lit on the streets below.

"You embarrassed me back there," Earl Sr. said without turning.

"I only asked a question." Chandler affirmed.

"You questioned my authority," Earl Sr. replied, "and worse, you did it in front of the men!"

"I asked the question *for* the men," Chandler said. "The reduction mandate affects them. AI will impact them."

"It affects *all* of us which is why we must be aligned." Earl Sr. turned sharply.

"Aligned with what?" Chandler asked. "With a memorandum that threatens fines and penalties for doing the work we've done our whole lives?"

"You're being sentimental." Earl Sr.'s expression hardened. His words were said in a mocking way.

"Then why does it feel wrong?" Chandler shot back before he could stop himself. "Why do you fear Vale?"

"This is not fear." Earl Sr. got within inches of Chandler's face. "This is adaptation. The world moves forward whether we approve of it or not."

"Who gets to choose the pace of how fast the world moves, though?" Chandler asked.

"Certainly not you," he reprimanded. "We will move at the pace that keeps us relevant. The Bliss name will not become a relic because of you!"

"And the men, who speaks for them?" Chandler swallowed.

"They will follow orders," Earl Sr. said firmly. "They will be compensated while they do. If they don't like it, there's the door." He pointed.

"You... You already knew about Artificial Illumination. You didn't hesitate to start chanting. You had already met with Mayor Pembroke and already agreed to the mandate yesterday," Chandler declared.

"You're damn right I did," Earl Sr. replied without hesitation.

"Before speaking to any of us?" Chandler braced himself, anticipating a potential backhanded strike from his grandfather.

"I didn't need to speak to any of you," Earl Sr. said. "I don't need anyone's permission to make decisions."

"What if you are wrong?" asked Chandler.

Earl Sr.'s gaze did not waver, as he puffed out his chest before responding. "Leadership requires unpleasant choices and taking risks," he proclaimed.

Chandler didn't know what to say. He thought of Pike counting wicks last night, of Travis's clenched jaw when he was being talked down to minutes ago. He thought about Miss Leslie, a local vendor who sold scented candles while sitting at her stall. Lastly, he remembered the candle that had refused to stay lit that morning.

"This plan is not about us prospering," Chandler said, more to himself than anyone else.

"What did you say?" Earl Sr. frowned, indignantly.

“Pembroke was not asking you for alignment,” Chandler met his grandfather’s eyes. “He was asking you for permission yesterday.”

“Permission for what?” scoffed Earl Sr.

“To replace *us*! To end *us*!” Chandler replied.

“You’re tired. You’ve been awake too long.” Earl Sr. chuckled.

“Maybe,” Chandler replied. “But...”

Earl Sr. stepped closer, interrupting Chandler before he could speak. He lowered his voice. “You listen to me carefully. AI is not our enemy, and resistance will not be tolerated. Maybe you are not the leader I thought.”

His grandfather’s words cut deeper than any knife. The insult crushed him. Across the hall, Pike, oblivious to the intensity of the conversation, let out a loud sneeze. The sound felt painfully out of place.

“Go home, kid, and get some rest. You’ll see this more clearly tomorrow.” Earl Sr. straightened his coat.

Chandler watched his grandfather walk away. He wasn’t so sure a good night’s sleep would make a difference; however, he’d been awake thirty-six hours. Maybe his exhaustion was simply clouding his judgment. Maybe AI wasn’t as alarming as it felt. After all, his grandfather and father believed in it and he trusted them. For tonight, that was enough.

A Necessary Adjustment

The first AI lampposts went up on SE 5th Street, close to Woodbine Avenue and only a block from the Bliss Candle Factory. Chandler noticed them on his way to work when the sun was barely peeking over the horizon. At first there was one; now a second stood farther down the street. The old posts with candles lay in a heap, a piece of board on top of them bearing writing:

Above a baker's doorway on James Street, a new AI fixture had been bolted to the brick. The wrought-iron bracket that used to hold three candles lay on the ground. It was bent in half and appeared vandalized. The candles were gone.

Chandler slowed as he walked past them. The street felt unfamiliar under his boots. He looked less at the shopfronts he'd known since boyhood and more at the new lamps.

The first one he'd seen had unsettled him. The second changed the whole tone of the street. Where the wood-and-iron posts had once stood like old companions, these new poles looked narrow and bare. They had clean lines and smooth joints from top to bottom. Their glass domes caught the morning light with a faint, cold sheen, more like ice than glass.

A man stood at the base of the nearest AI lamppost with his back to the street. Chandler didn't recognize him at first. The coat did look familiar, though. It was dark wool, patched at the elbow, and the stitches were fraying. A long pole with a brass hook was lying on the ground at his feet.

"Mr. Boone?" Chandler guessed.

The man turned slowly. His face brightened upon seeing Chandler, but then he grimaced as if he were in a bitter mood.

"Master Bliss," Boone replied, clearing his throat. "I didn't expect to see you. It's been years."

Rocky Boone had been a lamplighter for as long as Chandler could remember. As a boy, Chandler had watched him make his evening rounds of lighting the candles near Lincoln Boulevard, where

Bliss Manor was located. Boone always tipped his hat to children and had scolded Chandler a couple of times when he was a boy for running with friends down the sidewalks.

"What are you doing out on James Street?" Chandler asked.

Boone gestured his right hand toward the post. "I was relocated last week, but this is my last day on this street, too. The city told me I could finish the last couple of old lampposts over here, but after that..." He shrugged.

"After that?" Chandler pressed him to continue his sentence.

"They said I'm being reassigned," Boone replied, frowning. "Sanitation, removal of old lampposts and then I don't know, forced retirement, maybe. Vale has banned city workers from performing upkeep on anything that uses fire."

Chandler observed the broken look on his face, as if his world was falling apart. Boone had been a lamplighter since before Chandler was born. They both looked around at the few remaining candle lampposts, all of them marked for removal. A single tear fell from Boone's eye.

"I know you will miss this," Chandler empathized.

Boone nodded in agreement. "The funny thing is, I never thought about the candles much while I was lighting them. They were just... there, like old friends." He hesitated to share. "Vale told us that the city won't need men like us much longer."

Chandler had no reply or words of comfort. Boone picked up his pole and rested it against his shoulder. He let out a deep sigh and mourned the death of his profession.

"Great seeing you again, Master Chandler," Boone said, tipping his hat out of habit. "Please give Earl Sr. my best regards."

Chandler stood there, thinking. His conversation with Mr. Boone replayed in his head. Down the street, a shopkeeper struggled to remove a wrought-iron bracket outside his storefront. Three candles still sat in their holders. The man paused when Chandler approached.

"Good morning," the shopkeeper waved and then returned to his work.

"Good morning, sir," Chandler replied, although it saddened him to see the bracket being removed. "Need a hand, my friend?"

The man hesitated, his pride getting the best of him, then he nodded. Together they loosened the bolts. The metal squeaked and moaned as it came free. It must have weighed thirty pounds. The shopkeeper held the bracket awkwardly, staring at it. It was a stunning handmade piece of work.

"I didn't have to remove it," he mumbled. "They said it wasn't mandatory, yet."

"Yet?" Chandler prompted.

"I received a notice from a city courier, a friend, that my store's front was being converted to AI. To avoid paying future fines, I was encouraged to remove my old fixtures," he replied. "The courier wasn't supposed to tell me, but inspections are starting in a few months, and I can't afford the fines."

He lowered the fixture carefully to the ground. It was polished and well-kept. One of the candles tipped, fell on the ground, and rolled, stopping at Chandler's boot.

"My father made this," the shopkeeper pointed at the bracket. "He said a storefront should feel welcoming."

Chandler picked up the fallen candle and handed it back. He could tell that the shopkeeper was experiencing a mix of emotions. On one hand, the shopkeeper was excited about AI, but on the other, he felt like something was being lost. It was something he couldn't explain, but the change left a pit in his stomach.

"You should mount the fixture inside," Chandler offered his opinion. "Let the city monitor the outside. It's not like the inspectors are going to ever come inside."

"I wish I could, but customers expect AI now. Makes the place look... modern, I suppose." The man shook his head.

He carried the bracket inside without saying another word. Chandler watched through the window as the man set the bracket against the back wall, turning it so the candles faced inward, hidden from the view of the customers.

Children darted past Chandler, nearly knocking him over, laughing as they played. They ran to the new lamppost, stopping to stare up at it, hoping to see it turn on.

"Does it really turn on by itself?" one of them asked.

"No, dummy," another replied, teasing his friend. "My brother says there's a switch at City Hall."

"They are way better," a third child declared. "No matches or nasty smoke."

They began playing a game, pretending to flip invisible switches, shouting "on" and "off" as they ran. One of the boys yelled out that he was a candle coming to "burn your house down." He chased another kid around the street pretending to set the others on fire.

An older woman passed by frowning at them. "Mind yourselves," she scolded. "That's not something to joke about."

The children barely glanced at her before running off again, their laughter echoing down the street. Chandler watched them go, mocking and spitting on old lampposts that were laying as debris on the curb. Chandler stood there watching people as they walked. Some adults noticed the lamps, smiling, welcoming the change. Some adults frowned, missing the ways of old. The children didn't seem to care. They accepted that AI was the way of the future without giving it another thought.

A few women stepped out of a doorway, and one paused beneath a new AI lamppost that had just been set into the concrete. She covered her eyes, shading them though it wasn't even lit. Chandler assumed she was being silly, but she was putting on a show for her friends.

"It's brighter and better," she giggled.

"It's not even on," her companion laughed.

"Yes, and it's still better," she giggled again. "Out with the old and in with the new!"

Chandler continued walking, staying on the south side of town, as he passed another lamppost, then another. With each one, the city felt less like a place built by hands and more like something assembled. By the time he reached the corner, he realized he had not seen a single flame all morning.

He stopped beside one of the new lampposts and reached out to touch it. The metal was polished so well it showed no oily residue from his fingertips. He pulled his hand back after only a few seconds of touching the bulb. He didn't know why, but it felt wrong. Two older townsfolk walked past, talking as they went.

"Remarkable, aren't they?" one said.

"Progress always is, my friend," the other replied.

They kept walking and their happy-go-lucky cheer bothered Chandler more than he wanted to admit. They talked as if AI had always been there. Like the change was only natural and par for the course. People were taking to AI faster than he'd thought possible. He walked on, slower now.

Old scenes dashed through his memory and his mind continued to race. He thought of his father carrying him to the Covenant Festival under a sky full of hanging lanterns. Then, he remembered his grandfather explaining how a flame had guided their family through fog and rain. There was a vision of his late mother setting up a small candle by his bedside the first night he slept alone, telling him the light would keep him safe. It was the same candle he lit at her funeral and the same candle he kept in a secret hiding place.

Candlelight had always meant warmth and company. Candles embraced a person with love. The vibe from these new lampposts, even when they were off, felt cold. They were more like something that watched than something that welcomed. Near a tailor's storefront, two boys played a game of tossing pebbles at the base of a freshly-installed lamppost. Each stone struck with a piercing ding.

"Careful, boys," Chandler reminded them, "you don't want to damage it."

"My teacher says they're stronger than anything we had before." One of the boys grinned at him.

The boy said it with the certainty of someone who had never stopped to doubt or think critically for themselves. Chandler's stomach tossed again, like rabid monkeys were playing a game of hopscotch inside. It was April 10th and had been less than three weeks since the demonstration at City Hall, and already the youth had learned to admire AI. These boys treated the lampposts like they had earned their respect and appreciation. Chandler forced a smile and kept walking.

Down the road, the old candle street fixtures were piled in a wagon. There were toppled posts with bent brackets and cracked glass all over the place. A waxy residue clung in patches to the cobblestones. The lanterns had all been discarded. He could see where lamplighters' poles had rubbed the metal over years, leaving a smooth groove. He stepped closer and crouched, placing his fingers on a twisted candle fixture frame. The iron was warm from the sun and rough in his hands.

He remembered standing at his bedroom window as a boy, watching the lamplighter on his route. In fact, before he started in the factory, he, too, had done his fair share of lamp lighting. There had been a dignity to that work. It was a simple life of lifting a pole, coaxing a candle with a flame, and then watching the candle give light. A city worker walked toward him, pushing another cart of fixtures toward the heap.

"You're clearing them out this quickly?" Chandler asked.

"Orders from the mayor," the man said.

"But some of these lampposts were only installed a year ago." Chandler pointed to the pile of debris in the wagon.

"That's the point." The worker chuckled. "Faster we get this junk out of here, the fewer complaints we get."

Chandler stared at him and felt broken inside. The man meant no offense, but the words stung the same. Less than a month ago, candles were a thing of beauty. Today, they were garbage.

"Besides," the man added, "they say these old lamps are a risk now. These things are a public safety concern."

"A risk to public safety?" Chandler repeated.

"A fire hazard. You understand these things are silent killers," the worker said as he shrugged and moved on.

Chandler stepped away from the pile, feeling like he had interrupted a funeral. Mayor Pembroke and Vale were systematically erasing the memory of candles and had launched a public relations campaign against them. Across the street, the baker stood under his new AI light fixture, looking pleased. Flour dusted the front of his apron and the air smelled sweet.

"Morning, Chandler!" the baker called out. "Quite something, isn't it?"

"It is... different," Chandler responded.

"Different? It's wonderful. See how clean the sign looks? Our pastries look fresher already, and I don't have to crawl up a ladder every night. My back is grateful, and my wife is grateful to hear me stop complaining about my back," the baker laughed.

"It is... convenient," Chandler agreed. "Won't you miss the candles?"

"Candles are still good for birthday cakes, for a nice romantic supper, but not for business!" He pointed up. "AI is better by leaps and bounds." The baker smiled from ear to ear.

Chandler nodded in agreement, but the words hurt. Candles took effort, wax, time, and a steady hand. AI took none of that. What made his trade meaningful was the same thing that now made it easy to replace. A hard banging sound drew his attention. Across the street, two men from the city were unbolting a wrought-iron candle fixture from a seamstress's shop. The woman stood in the doorway holding up her hands.

"Please be careful," she said. "My husband made that candle fixture by hand for our thirtieth anniversary."

"We'll dispose of it properly, ma'am," one of the workers replied.

"Dispose of it?" she echoed. "Can we keep it?"

The workers carried the fixture toward the pile and smashed it on the ground. With tears in her eyes, the seamstress glanced around and caught Chandler's eye. The two of them looked at each other, no words, only the shared understanding that something important was being destroyed.

Chandler walked around the city for hours, fasting the entire day. He trudged around until the day gave way to night. He had never missed a day of work in his life, but today he did. The new lamps gleamed overhead like small moons, and they gave off no smoke. They had no smell or soot. As he walked on, he heard hammers farther down the street. Another post was being set. Another base was poured. Another patch of the city, forgetting its past.

Confirming Compliance

By the next week, the changes hit the north side of Main Street, where the market was located. After work, Chandler went there for dinner, as he routinely did, but the place felt wrong the moment he stepped under the arches. Crews were already at work taking the lanterns down from their hooks. Candles were stripped from posts and rolls of copper wire were stacked against the stone columns.

A shorter man from a rival candle shop conversed with several government officials from the Department of Industrial Development. The owner of the candle shop slipped the bureaucrat a handful of cash in hopes that his shop would get AI installed sooner.

Some vendors had hung signs out in front of their shops that said "**AI USED HERE.**" The light itself changed the look of the crowd. The AI lamps threw hard-edged shadows and cut people's faces into sharper shapes. People seemed brighter and clearer and, in some strange way, less human. Their smiles shone as they boasted about being among the first to use AI in their stores. To Chandler, they looked more like reflections of their former selves.

He stopped in the middle of the walkway and for a moment, it felt like someone had moved the market further away. He saw the same awnings, the usual stacked crates, and the brick walls of shops he had visited since boyhood, but it felt like he had never been there before. Several people brushed past, offering quick apologies. With the new light they could see better, but somehow not at all.

He'd grown up on these streets. As a boy, he'd run between tables with a loaf of bread under his arm and his father close behind. Lanterns had swung above the stalls. Now the lights overhead did not move. They stared straight down.

He turned toward a vendor's stall near the front edge of the market square. A woman, who made candles and sold them to give the proceeds to an orphanage, sat there. The sweet smell of scented candles had always hung thick in the air. As a child, he'd called it the sweet candle stand. The woman there had once given him a small, scented candle for free. He had carried it home in both hands like treasure. To this day, it was kept in a safe place in his small house.

Today, the wooden sign above the stall hung crooked and the shelves were half full. In their place, a roll of copper wire rested on the counter, along with a crate of AI bulbs. Near the back of the stall were about thirty candles, but they did not appear to be for sale. Miss Leslie stood behind the table with her hands folded; she appeared flustered.

Chandler stopped a few feet from the stall, unsure whether to speak or turn away. Miss Leslie dabbed at her eyes with a handkerchief and attempted to smile though it did not hold.

"I didn't expect to see you today," she said softly. "Most folks have been avoiding this corner."

"I still come this way," Chandler replied. "Old habits."

"Yes, habits." She giggled.

"They're still lovely." He pointed toward the few remaining candles.

"They always were," she said, then corrected herself. "They are, I mean."

For a moment they simply stood there, the sounds of the market pressing in around them, metal clinking, boots on stone, and the faint chatter of bargaining. Above them, an AI lamp hummed faintly, its light steady, cold, and unforgiving.

"They came early this morning," Miss Leslie sulked. "Two inspectors."

"I heard through the grapevine that inspections were not to start for a couple of months." Chandler scoffed, then began to speak critically of the inspectors.

"They were polite," she interrupted, defending them. "They asked permission before stepping behind the table and gave me several compliments about my displays. One of them even said my lavender smelled exquisite and that it reminded him of his mother's house."

Chandler stood there dumbfounded. Was she seriously defending the implementation of AI without giving it a passing thought of the consequences for her business?

"They had me complete a survey," she continued. "They asked me about my projected monthly productivity, quantity of the materials used, and the total of last month's revenue." She let out a shaky breath. "They told me open flame sales were 'under review,' and that I should begin transitioning immediately if I wanted to avoid penalties."

"Penalties?" Chandler repeated.

"They said it kindly." She nodded.

As if summoned, two men approached the stall. They wore clean coats and carried clipboards tucked under their arms. One adjusted his thick-framed glasses as he walked. The other smiled, greeting others as he approached.

"Miss Leslie," the taller one said pleasantly. "We're making a final pass on our way back to City Hall."

"Of course," she replied, straightening the rows of candles. "How can I help you fine gentlemen?" she gestured toward the man with spectacles. "Did you find that bouquet for your wife you mentioned earlier?"

They did not look at Chandler, intentionally not making eye contact. That was until Miss Leslie started the introductions.

"This is Master Chandler Bliss," she said. "He's like family to me."

"Ah," one inspector said, extending a hand. "A pleasure to meet you, Chandler."

They cordially shook hands like gentlemen. One of the inspectors was a middle-aged handsome man. Miss Leslie was not married, and the inspector did not have on a wedding ring. It was cute to watch Miss Leslie attempt to flirt while remaining coy.

"We won't take much time," the married inspector said. "We must confirm compliance."

"Those will, unfortunately, need to be disposed of," he glanced at the candles at the back of the stall. "All vendors that deal in candles must follow the seventy-percent reduction orders, no exceptions."

"I have those candles reserved for the orphanage," she said, batting her eyes. "Sister Mary will be here later to pick them up."

"We're sorry, ma'am," he pointed to his clipboard, showing her a neat list of monetary fine amounts for violations. "Rules are rules!"

"Yes, I understand. I will dispose of them," she reluctantly agreed as she was fearful of a fine.

"Excellent," the handsome inspector said, making a note. "The city appreciates cooperation and so do I."

Chandler stepped forward. "Is there any allowance for charity donations?" he asked. "These candles light the orphanage on Hope Street."

The inspectors exchanged a brief look and chatted between themselves about the legality of the request. They didn't seem to fully agree, as the handsome inspector tried to find a loophole in the stack of paperwork on his clipboard.

"There are grants available," the other inspector replied. "An application may be submitted at City Hall."

"And until then?" Chandler pressed him.

The other inspector smiled apologetically. "Until then, regulations apply equally. I am terribly sorry, ma'am." He tipped his hat to Miss Leslie and they both moved on, already on their way back to City Hall.

Miss Leslie's shoulders sagged once they were gone. She let out a long sigh, glancing at the candles that were promised to the orphanage.

"Well, it's not all of my candles I must dispose of. That's a plus, right?" She forced a joyless laugh. "It's only a temporary mandate," she went on. "Things will settle back to normal once AI is implemented."

"No! No, they won't," Chandler raised his voice and immediately wished he hadn't.

She looked at him, her eyes full of despair. Chandler felt terrible for borderline yelling but listening to the foolishness of her comments was too much. Regardless, he had no right to be cruel or unloving. Miss Leslie was not the one that was restricting candles or anything to do with flames.

"You're with the Bliss family!" she shouted. "Surely there's something you can do about this?"

The weight of Chandler's last name settled on his shoulders, a feeling he was more than familiar with.

"I can speak to my grandfather," he said. "I can try."

"That would be fantastic." Her face lit with gratitude.

Chandler reached into his coat pocket and pulled out his wallet. He placed a significant amount of money on the counter, more than the price of any candle.

"No." She pushed his hand back, refusing to accept the money.

"For the orphanage when Sister Mary arrives," he said.

Miss Leslie wept. She was one of the finest scented candle makers in Hanover, rivaling only the Bliss Candle Factory, of course. It was devastating to see her cry and not be able to comfort her.

"I'm sorry," he said. "Truly!"

"So am I," another tear rolled down her face.

He stepped away from the stall. Behind him, Miss Leslie began packing the candles for the orphanage into a crate. She was careful, deliberate, as though preparing them for sleep rather than their demise.

Chandler meandered through the market, stopping at a couple of shops. By the time he reached the far side of the market square, multiple pairs of new inspectors had already arrived, the two closest were speaking with a baker beneath an old candle fixture mounted to his stall. The baker nodded along, smiling, unaware of how closely he resembled Miss Leslie only an hour earlier.

Chandler wandered back over to Miss Leslie's store as it was on his way home. Her stall stood quieter now, its strong scent fading into the air. The orphanage would go dark sooner than anyone realized if her candle sales stopped.

"Good afternoon, again, Miss Leslie," Chandler joked, as if he had not just seen her.

"Master Chandler," she played along, "I didn't think you still came this way."

"I do," he smiled, "or should I say did?" His eyes moved over her empty racks. "You're closing for the night?"

"No, I am not *closing*," she had regained her composure. She answered with a short, dry laugh.

Metal scraped hard against stone somewhere behind him. The baker's candle fixture came crashing down while the inspectors barked orders at the demolition crew. Chandler flinched at the sound. Miss Leslie had almost finished packing up all the candles at her booth, not just the ones marked for disposal.

"If you'd like," Chandler inquired politely, "I can come back tomorrow and help you sell the remaining candles?"

"That is kind, but there's no need," she replied. "Two different inspectors stopped by already and they bought my whole inventory. I'm required to hand all of them over at the end of the week for disposal. They'll compensate me at full price."

The word *compensate* sounded flat and heavy in her mouth. Chandler pictured full boxes of perfectly good candles loaded into a wagon and hauled away to be burned or buried. His stomach churned with despair.

"Do you remember the thunderstorm six years ago," he asked, "when the wind destroyed most of the candle fixtures in town?"

Her eyes lifted. "It was horrible," she said. "The square went dark."

"You gave away every spare candle you had and sent me running to the food stalls," Chandler grinned. "You refused to take a single dollar for reimbursement."

Miss Leslie's shoulders loosened as the memory took hold. Chandler could see that she was reminiscing about the thunderstorm and taking care of her fellow citizens of Hanover, the city that she loved.

"You came back soaked to the bone," she teased, "and the whole market wondered who this boy was handing out candles." A real smile crept across her face. "Oh, and the puddles all looked like they were filled with stars," she giggled.

Chandler certainly did remember it. For a while that night, it had seemed like the square was lit with a million candles. Now white bars from the AI lamps shone on the damp patches of stone. They didn't dance because they lacked life. They were just there, sharp and still.

"Things do change, Master Chandler," Miss Leslie smiled. "They always have and always will. We moved from tallow to beeswax, from lousy wicks to better ones. Maybe AI is that, another type of... wick."

"A wick still burns," he replied with passion. "It gives itself up to the flame."

She looked at him for a long moment, then bent over to reach far under the counter. When she stood upright, she set a small glass jar in front of him. A candle sat inside it, lopsided. Wax had spilled over one edge.

"This one never made it to the shelf," she said. "The pour went wrong. I was going to melt it down. Consider it my last mistake."

"I can't take this..." Chandler insisted.

"You can," she urged. "They can pay me for the rest, but not for this. Take it, please. Let it burn somewhere when they're not watching."

His throat tightened as he picked up the jar. It was imperfect, but lovely. The faint smudge of her thumb was still visible on the glass.

"Thank you," Chandler wiped a tear from under his left eye.

He stepped away from the stall with the little candle cupped in his hand, bidding farewell to Miss Leslie. The noise of the market rushed back in, horses neighing, metal hammering, men shouting orders, and some fool laughing too loudly from a strong drink.

At the entrance to the market, a banner stretched across a booth run by men in city uniforms. The banner said, "**AI USED HERE.**" Under it, a polished pole held a bulb and there was a discounted price on it. The fixture was designed for bedrooms or kitchens. One of Vale's engineers turned it on and off while a crowd watched. Each burst of light drew excitement from the prospective buyers.

"Look at that," someone near Chandler gasped, "makes the old lanterns look like children's toys."

"About time we caught up with the world," a woman added.

Chandler heard every word they said. He thought of birthdays, weddings, vigils, all held under candlelight. He had to force his jaw to unclench. He didn't smash the AI bulbs though the thought did cross his mind. He did nothing as the jar from Miss Leslie warmed his palm from his grip.

At some point, he drifted out of the square, though he had no desire to head home. The AI fixtures buzzed faintly above James Street. People walked beneath them without so much as a glance.

Chandler stopped under one of the new street lamps and looked up. His reflection was warped across the glass. He lifted the candle from Miss Leslie, so both appeared in the curve of the dome, the small handmade light and the cold, perfect sphere, and then he looked away.

PART II

"The Alignment"

Under Observation

Chandler didn't walk to the factory the next morning; he ran. By the time he reached the door, his lungs burned. He went straight to his workbench, set his tools down, and began arranging them in their usual places. Wick trimmers were set near the front of the table. The ladles were placed to the right side, and the molds were neatly arranged to his left.

The motions of doing something normal soothed him. It was Saturday, his last day in the factory before the Sabbath. Tomorrow, thankfully, he would be in church, singing, praying, and worshiping Jesus. He started to work, trying hard not to think about AI.

Travis, his old friend, sat at a work bench nearby. Chandler nodded at him and uttered, "Good morning." Moments later, he felt someone watching him. A mysterious woman he didn't recognize sat at the table across from his bench. She was not a candlemaker or an apprentice. She simply sat there, hands folded, eyes fixed on him. She'd been waiting for him to arrive.

"You hear the news?" she asked, breaking the silence with a gentle tone of voice. "AI is being installed in this building today. The engineers came in during the night and have already started preparing. It's wonderful news. right?"

"I hadn't heard," Chandler replied. "I thought we weren't scheduled for AI until next year." He forced a polite smile.

"Earl Bliss Sr. had a word with Mayor Pembroke," she said with a smile, but she was not necessarily polite. "Your grandfather was concerned that other factories would receive AI before yours."

"I did hear him mention that a couple times." Chandler didn't know what to say and the conversation felt awkward.

"The mayor agreed and before the end of today, Artificial Illumination will be shining in here, as well. Now, I'll ask you again. It's wonderful news, isn't it?"

The factory wasn't loud, but suddenly every sound felt exaggerated. Chandler could hear every noise, every clink of metal on copper, stools scraping the floor, and apprentices chatting by the racks. Travis, overhearing the conversation, had lifted his head to listen, but he didn't say anything. Chandler swallowed hard.

"I suppose many would say it's *promising*," he replied.

"Promising," she repeated. "Such a careful word for such a bright future, sir."

"I'm a candlemaker, ma'am. We are not known for elegant words. All I know is how wax sets." He forced a small laugh.

"Oh, I think the wax has already set," she declared, playfully. "Most people simply haven't noticed yet."

A chill went up his neck. He wasn't sure if she meant the trade of candlemaker, the city of Hanover, or something else altogether. He noticed her hands. She wore gloves made of fine silk. There was no wax or soot on them. She didn't look like anyone who had ever trimmed a wick. Why was she here? Her fingers tapped gently on the table as if she were waiting for a signal.

"Well, don't you agree?" she asked again. "AI is wonderful news, right?"

She stood and walked behind him. Her eyes flicked briefly over his shoulder toward the center of the hall. He resisted the urge to turn toward her. Somewhere behind him a conversation cut off mid-sentence. An apprentice stopped humming and making small talk with his assigned mentor. Near the factory offices, he could hear laughter abruptly stop. The woman waited patiently for Chandler to respond. Suddenly, the whole room was listening.

"AI is certainly remarkable," Chandler turned to face her. "The world seems eager for it."

"Eager?" she parroted. "And what about you, Master Chandler? Are *you* eager for AI?"

His mind flooded with anxiety for he hadn't told her his name. Of course, she knew it, everyone in Hanover knew the Bliss family. Their candles had lit Hanover for generations, long before Vale and his AI bulbs.

There was something about the way she said "Master Chandler" that didn't sit right. She spoke with precision and was deliberate with her words, as if she had read his name off a list.

"I try to be grateful for whatever the mayor thinks is best for Hanover," Chandler said. "If he believes AI will help the city, then I'm sure it has its place."

"Such loyalty to the mayor," she commended. "Hanover is fortunate to have you."

Chandler grabbed another candle to keep his hands busy. He used his tools and the wick cutter. He straightened a ladle that didn't need straightening, anything to avoid her stare. From the entrance, the heavy doors opened and shut. Men's voices carried inside. They were official tones, like lawyers speaking to the jury. It was the kind of voices that read decrees and verdicts. He peered at the entrance, but no one was there.

"You must feel proud," the woman went on, regaining Chandler's attention.

"Proud? Why is that?" he paused while working.

"To be here, of course," she proclaimed. "The Bliss Candle Factory, one of the first trades to be fully integrated with AI. To be *observed*, I mean *honored*, by the Department of Industrial Development." She coughed as she corrected herself with a small smile. "Your family company stands at the line between old and new. History will remember you, Chandler."

The word *observed* landed with a direct impact and Chandler didn't hear much after she said it. He imagined eyes on the rafters, watching him. He pondered reports being written with his name underlined in red. It was a foolish thought, but it wouldn't leave his mind.

"History remembers kings," Chandler replied, trying to sound nonchalant, "not candlemakers."

"On the contrary, Chandler," she said. "History is being rewritten all the time. Old names move down the page and new ones replace them on the first line. Sometimes all it takes is a sentence change and someone willing to make the edits."

He had no idea what she meant, but it sounded godlike, what she was describing. Near the offices, someone laughed hysterically. The timing of their laugh made things worse. The laughter happened quickly, loudly, and then stopped at once. It sounded like the laughter was on cue with the woman's remarks.

"You feel it, don't you?" the woman asked, pointing. "The change, Chandler. It's like a refreshing draft under that door."

"I feel many things," Chandler declared, "but feelings don't count for much."

"You speak like a man who's already chosen sides." She gave a small, dry chuckle.

She tapped the table twice with a gloved finger. He half-expected her to pull out a notebook and start writing, but she didn't. The only thing she did was stare at him, studying his body language. He acted unaffected, though his eyes betrayed him.

"Tell me, Master Bliss," she said, lowering her voice. "What did *you* see at the City Hall demonstration?"

How did she know he went? He looked around, his heart was beating a million times a minute. The enormous factory felt small, like the walls were closing in around him. He positioned himself to move towards Travis, but she countered him and moved directly in the path.

"I saw the same thing everyone else saw," he replied.

"But we don't all see the same thing, do we?" she asserted. "Some saw their future, and some saw a funeral."

Miss Leslie's stall at the market flashed in his mind, and the way she cried, mourning the death of her business. His hand twitched and his chest tightened.

"I saw a demonstration," he said. "Nothing more."

"Did it please you?" she asked.

"It impressed me," he admitted. "And it unsettled me in my spirit."

"Unsettled, why unsettled?" Her eyes sharpened.

"Because it was so bright," he forced another laugh. "You could barely see the person next to you. The brightness unsettled me, that's all."

She gave a small, satisfied nod. "Sometimes brightness hides as much as it reveals."

He couldn't tell whether she agreed with him or if she was taking notes in her head. He glanced up at the walls and noticed faint chalk marks dotting the beams and plaster. The engineers must have put them there. Until this point, he had not noticed them, but now each mark looked like a claim. Put a new AI fixture here and remove the old candle fixtures.

"You'll be surprised how quickly a workplace can be transformed once AI is there," she leaned in, whispering. "One moment you recognize it, the next, you can hardly remember how you ever worked without it. Let's not forget that you will be safer, as well."

Safety again. Chandler was so tired of hearing that word tossed around. The word used to mean trimmed wicks, clear walkways, and keeping lamps away from curtains. Now it meant something different. Labeling something as "for safety" was merely a bid for control.

"You talk as if it's already done," Chandler said.

"In some ways, it is," she tilted her head. "Decisions were made before the first wire came through your doors."

The hairs on his arms rose as anger pulsed through his body. Every instinct told him to walk away, but he couldn't for fear of harming the Bliss Candle Factory's reputation, or worse, damaging his grandfather's good name. The woman stood there, again in uncomfortable silence. She blinked occasionally, but her eyes never left Chandler.

"There are many eyes on this place, Master Bliss," she added. "Important people are interested in how the Bliss Candle Factory adjusts to AI. It is crucial that we see a smooth transition." She held his gaze, staring into his soul. "We must know who helps and who hinders."

"Then I suppose we'd better adjust to AI," Chandler affirmed as the words tasted bitter on his tongue.

"It would be unwise not to," she agreed. "Tell me, do you ever worry your candles might be misunderstood?"

“Misunderstood how? They are candles!” Chandler shrugged.

“As symbols,” she mirrored his body language. “Men do foolish things in the dark. A candle in a certain window, on a certain night, could mean... anything. A message or a signal. Or perhaps a way to gather. Can you imagine?”

Chandler thought of the stubborn candle on the reception desk that wouldn’t stay lit. Pike had called it a sign. A candle was a candle; it was not a sign of defiance.

“I make candles so people can see,” he said. “To sew at night. To read stories to children. To pray to God, that’s all.”

“For now,” she winked.

A tool fell off a shelf and tumbled to the floor nearby. The clang echoed longer than it should have. The man who had dropped it apologized urgently; he was afraid not to. Other candlemakers were still watching, although they pretended they were not.

“You have a choice,” the woman went on, raising her voice. “All of you candlemakers do. You can treat AI as an enemy, or you can treat it as a partner.”

“And if we decide it’s just... there?” Chandler asked. “Not an enemy, not a partner, but just there.”

“Then we will decide for you,” she smiled.

Footsteps approached from the far side of the hall. The woman's expression shifted to a peppy smile. She adjusted her gloves, smoothed her skirt, and fluffed her hair. She giggled and became flirtatious in her demeanor.

"I hope, Master Bliss," she said, giggling, "that you'll be on the right side of history when this is finished."

"The right side?" he asked.

"There are only two now," she smiled. "Those who help Hanover shine and those who cast shadows on it."

Her eyes lingered on him long enough to make the point. She turned her attention away, already moving toward another group of workers. Chandler's shoulders were rigid and he had not taken a breath for over a minute. His hands shook. He hovered over his tools as if he'd forgotten what to do with them. He drew a slow breath, bracing for whatever those approaching footsteps would bring. He'd never felt so alone.

Activation

Pike's voice cut through his thoughts. It was Pike's footsteps Chandler had heard.

"Master Chandler, sir!" Pike embraced him.

The woman was already on the other side of the factory as Pike reached the bench. As she turned, Chandler caught sight of a small pin on her handbag. It was the eye and torch logo from the banners at City Hall. She had crossed the room to greet other workers by their first names, slipping into conversation as if she'd never been speaking to Chandler at all.

"Today's order list, sir," Pike handed Chandler a single sheet of paper.

Normally, the list ran to dozens of pages. Today it was barely half a page. Sales had dropped far beyond the seventy percent cut Director Vale had ordered. Candles hadn't vanished entirely, but fewer people came by to buy them. When they did, they spoke in low voices, like customers buying something they didn't want their neighbors to see. The old constant stream of patrons was gone.

Regarding the factory's profits, Earl Jr. had claimed multiple times in the past week that they had never looked better. The money from the city's reimbursement arrived on schedule. Wages were paid and men celebrated that they could leave early. Some of them didn't even put on aprons anymore. Instead, they played cards at their benches and wandered outside more often. On paper, everything was fine.

A demolition crew and a team of engineers arrived not long after Pike did, like they'd been standing outside waiting for a signal. The woman with the eye-and-torch pin hurried to the front doors and greeted them by their first names.

Earl Sr. and several other Bliss family members came down from their offices, smiling broadly as they shook hands. Earl Jr. pointed out various fixtures along the walls. There was no ceremony to it. The engineers and laborers simply started tearing them down.

Industrial chandeliers that had hung there for decades were wrenched free and tossed into bins. Glass lanterns clinked and cracked. One of the workers knocked a candle off a shelf. When it hit the floor, the man smirked, and brought his boot down hard. The wax crushed flat under his heel. The mysterious woman with the pin laughed hysterically.

Chandler stared at the pale smear on the floor. For a second he couldn't move. He'd seen candles break before, of course. Molds that went wrong were thrown away. Wicks that tunneled or were too thin were burned in the furnaces. There were mistakes and certainly candles that never made it out of the factory. However, even the worst batches were handled with care and respect. The "bad" candles were melted down and given another chance to be useful. He had never watched someone intentionally *stomp* a candle out of existence like that, as if they were proving a point.

"Master Chandler... will they take down all the fixtures?" Pike shifted nervously beside him.

"It seems so," Chandler replied.

Pike nodded but looked as though he had seen a ghost. His eyes followed the crew as they moved along the walls, barely glancing at what they destroyed. Every time a flame was extinguished, the factory grew darker. To the laborers it was plaster, metal, and relics from the past. The fixtures were not works of art, not worthy of their respect. The fixtures were a burden. They were garbage. They were treated like filth.

Another fixture came free with a sharp crack. The worker flung it into the bin. The growing pile clattered and rattled with every new piece. Chandler made his way toward the central aisle. The engineers worked in practiced rhythm, passing tools, calling for wire, and marking additional points along the beams. Their faces showed no hesitation, no particular interest. This was just another building on an extensive list of work to be completed.

"Do they even know how these fixtures and candles were made? My father used to say those brass molds came from England. Do they know that Robert Earl Bliss, one of the city's founding fathers, carried them on a ship to the new world?" Pike asked, his fingers fidgeting.

"That's true; he sure did," Chandler affirmed. "Those specific fixtures are still up in the loft."

"Will they take those, too?" Pike asked.

Chandler didn't respond. He couldn't. Pike dropped the conversation as he noticed it was bothering Chandler. Around them, the other candlemakers hovered at the edges of their workbenches. Some relaxed, sat down, folded their arms, and leaned back against their benches. Others stood straight, faces blank with no emotion, as if they were not there at all. A few of the older men stared at the floor. They pretended they didn't notice the changes.

"We're not allowed to make candles while the engineers are here," someone mentioned. "They said it would interfere with the installation process."

“Them being in the factory is interfering with us more than anything,” another replied, covering his mouth so as not to be seen speaking.

No one dared to speak above the volume of a whisper and the air in the factory felt different. Chandler paused by his bench. The wood was worn smoothly where his hands had rested over the years. Flecks of old wax clung in the grooves. A streak of lavender marked the spot from last Easter’s order of candles for Covenant Cathedral. He ran his fingers along the grain, feeling the memories of his old life flash before his eyes.

At the far end of the hall, the crew reached the last line of candle fixtures. Their movements were graceful, yet horribly destructive. They were like a group of stagehands dismantling a stage after a play. All the memories of previous generations, all the men who had stood under those fixtures before, who had trimmed a million wicks, who had laughed and shed tears, it all meant nothing now.

“Master Chandler, look.” Pike was passionately pointing at the engineers.

Near the back wall, Travis, standing at 6’5″, his beard permanently splattered with wax, stood in front of a candle fixture he’d tended for years. He didn’t move as he towered over the engineers. His hands shook with anger as he stood in their way.

“Sir, you’ll need to step aside,” the engineer gave clear direction.

Travis didn't answer.

"Sir, our orders are to remove all candle fixtures. You'll need to step to the side, now!"

Travis didn't answer. The woman reached into her bag and pulled out a small journal. She began writing a note, presumably about Travis's refusal to move. Chandler noticed and started striding toward the engineer.

"It's all right, brother." Chandler went to Travis and put a hand on his shoulder.

Travis, trusting Chandler, gave a small nod and stepped away. His legs moved, but his eyes stayed on the fixture until the worker twisted it loose. The metal groaned as it came free. Travis flinched as it dropped into the bin with the rest. Travis turned and walked away without a word. Chandler had never seen him look so small. The woman giggled.

Up front, Earl Jr. spoke loudly with the engineers. They joked, laughed, and patted each other on the backs like old friends. Bottles of champagne sat on ice. He handed each of the engineers and laborers a cigar.

"Less than two hours to do the whole building? Gentlemen, your work is truly remarkable." Earl Jr. lit a long cigar. "Think of the gains you have helped us with today. No more relighting, no more shifting shadows, and you have increased the safety for our hard-working team. This will transform our production capabilities."

"Glorious efficiency," Earl Sr. boasted. "Efficiency is the blood of industry. The Bliss legacy will grow beyond what two hours ago we ever thought was possible."

Chandler watched them and he tried not to gag. His grandfather and father were pleased, excited, and enthusiastic about AI. Whatever they felt about the factory, it certainly wasn't loss or despair. They were blind to what was being taken away as they could only see the promise of what *might* be added.

New sleek fixtures, plated in silver and stamped discreetly with the eye-and-torch symbol, went up where old ones had been. Wires were threaded through the rafters like veins. Every time a wire was connected, a faint hum traveled along the beams. Chandler reached toward one of the new brackets, but he stopped a few inches short. The metal was polished and he could see his reflection. He looked like the shadow of death had visited him.

He thought of the old fixtures, crooked, handmade, and each different. Several of his ancestors had dedicated hours of their lives to making them. They'd held thousands of flames over the years. These new fixtures didn't look like they were meant to hold anything.

"Chandler?" Travis uttered.

"Yes?" Chandler held back tears.

“Do you think AI will replace the whole factory someday? All of us?” Travis asked.

Chandler tried to open his mouth, but his tongue was paralyzed against his teeth. He looked Travis in the eyes. Both stared at each other, waiting for the other to say something.

“Our work has survived a lot,” Chandler wiped his eyes. “Wars. Food shortages. Hard years and good years. We’re still here. AI changes a lot, but it doesn’t change who we are.”

Chandler earnestly wished that he believed the words he spoke to Travis, but he didn’t. He felt a duty as a Bliss to calm Travis’s nerves. The demolition crew was rolling the bins of disposed fixtures toward the rear doors of the factory. The terrible noise coming from the bins, the fixtures being tossed around, sounded like demons being cast into hell.

“They’re taking everything from us,” cried Travis.

Chandler looked at the piles of metal and broken glass in the bins. There were marks left on the walls where the old fixtures had been. Now, there were empty spaces resembling scars on the factory’s walls.

“I know,” Chandler put his arm around Travis.

When the crew finished removing the last bin, they turned their full attention to the new system. The factory looked bare as only light came through the windows now. The warm flames that had once lined the walls were gone. The only thing remaining was raw brick and wooden beams.

“Breaker is ready. Prepare for activation.” The head engineer raised his voice.

A low hum started at the far wall, deepening as they tested the connections. Chandler felt vibrations in his boots. The candlemakers all stopped talking as their attention shifted. They were all watching. Earl Jr. stepped back as he continued to smoke his cigar. Samuel trembled and Chandler stood there with a blank look on his face.

“Initiating Illumination!” one of the engineers exclaimed.

Chandler took a breath and held it. The switch was thrown to the on position. For a heartbeat, nothing happened at all. A moment later, the factory flooded with intense light. The light poured from the new fixtures in a bright, flat luminescence that reached into every corner. There was no flickering whatsoever. The entire factory, the racks, the stains on the floor, everything stood out in sharp detail. It was like seeing the factory for the first time and not recognizing it at all.

The Inspection

Two men, wearing fancy clothes, arrived not long after the new fixtures came on. Both men were dressed in matching dark slacks, crisp white shirts, and their shoes were spotless. They strolled through the doorway with confidence, like men who expected respect without needing to earn it. They bore blue armbands with the eye-and-torch logo wrapped around their sleeves. Each man carried a clipboard.

Chandler was kneeling beside a fresh crate of frankincense-scented candles. He was sorting them by size and shade. He looked up when the men started pointing in his direction, motioning him over. They stood beside Earl Sr., Earl Jr., and several of Chandler's uncles. The group was deep in conversation. There were no smiles now.

"You must be young Master Chandler," one of the men assumed, as Chandler approached. "Director Vale wanted to be sure you were included in our conversations."

"Yes, I'm Chandler, and you are?" Chandler wiped his hands on his apron.

“We represent the Council of Illumination,” the first man replied. “It is a branch of the Department of Industrial Development. We have been tasked with overseeing all AI implementation.”

“The Bliss Candle Factory is at the top of our list,” the second man added. “Now that you are using AI, your factory has been selected for a routine compliance review, pursuant to Article Four of the AI Transition Mandate. We are inspectors.”

“Well then, let’s get on with it,” the other inspector said, eyeing Chandler. “What do you think of AI, son?”

Chandler chose his words carefully as he looked around. He was not about to make the same mistake he had made with the mysterious woman earlier that day. Or at least, he prayed, he would avoid embarrassing his family again. He decided to paraphrase what he had already heard his father say as it seemed to be acceptable.

“There are advantages… The light, the light… it is steady and keeps production from stop-stopping to tend wicks or relight la-lamps.” Chandler responded, stuttering his words.

The first inspector wrote down every word as though Chandler were dictating a confession. The second inspector had already begun to roam, his eyes skating across shelves and ledgers, counting boxes, opening cabinets, checking the racks. He hardly paused long enough to see what he was looking at.

Chandler watched him move aimlessly. The man never truly studied anything. His gaze merely slid over the factory. He examined the factory the same way a surveyor might glance over land he already planned to divide. Racks, tools, rows of candles, bottles filled with oil, all of it was something to be measured and judged by the inspector.

He stopped beneath one of the new AI fixtures and tilted his head enough for the bulb's glare to wash across his clipboard. The metal casing above his head bore the eye-and-torch emblem as it had been stamped deep into the steel. That mark was like a fungus growing on the city since it had first been displayed on the banners at City Hall. Now it was on lapel pins, walls, street corners, and worse, on the lights in Chandler's own workplace.

The inspector's shadow stretched across the floorboards. As he moved back towards them, the shadow of the eye-and-torch slid across benches and tools. The shadow fell over old wax stains and carved initials, crawling across the factory like an evil spirit.

He flipped a page on his clipboard, revealing a stack of identical forms. The forms had multiple tiny boxes and narrow lines for signatures. "We will, of course," he said to Earl Jr., "need Form 3-

23C, Sub-Addendum for Unintended Warming Artifacts," he pulled a manual from his pocket and examined it carefully, "unless your facility qualifies for a Certified Thermal Exemption, that is. Are you categorized as an 11-21 or 11-21T?"

"I don't believe we were given those categories or have seen those forms before," Earl Jr. said, blinking rapidly.

The inspector sighed, as if personally disappointed with Earl Jr.'s response. Chandler and the rest of his family stood there, listening.

"All facilities awaiting AI installment were notified two days ago," the inspector scolded him. "Failure to comply with pre-compliance is a violation of compliance, naturally, a violation of Article Six, Subsection Eight-2." He slid another paper from his stack, this one printed with bold red letters on top. "You'll need to sign the Non-Intentional Non-Compliance Acknowledgment. Two signatures are required, and I will sign as a witness to notarize the warning."

He set the form carefully atop a smaller sheet labeled Receipt of Provisional Intent to Acknowledge Receipt. Candlemakers were not known for stacks of paperwork. At most, the factory operated on inventory sheets and the only thing ever requiring a signature were invoices verifying a delivery had been completed.

"But..." the inspector added, "you may not sign until we verify your eligibility to sign." He scanned the room. "Where is your Signatory Verification Officer? A factory this size must have one or two depending on your staff-to-square-footage ratio."

"Everyone, get back to work," Earl Sr. instructed the group of candlemakers who had gathered listening to the conversation. He smiled and explained, "This is a routine review now that we have been blessed with AI and there is nothing to worry about."

His right hand pointed toward their workbenches, and his face scowled at them. The workers, including Chandler and his uncles, went back to their tasks, but the easy rhythm of the factory was gone. Men who could have poured wax and trimmed wicks in their sleep now carefully measured each motion. Even the most tenured candlemakers were suddenly aware of how they stood and how they held their tools. All conversations died and common joke-telling gave way to tight-lipped, stoic faces.

Chandler's posture stiffened. He straightened up tall and smoothed his apron as he was afraid of looking idle. Per the direction of his grandfather, he started his walk back to his workbench. The first inspector walked closely beside Chandler, their sleeves brushing. When they arrived at his workbench, Chandler resumed his normal tasks.

The inspector's pen moved across the page as he watched, but his face showed no real interest. His pen moved calmly until Chandler hesitated to begin a task, then his hand wrote aggressively.

"What would you say, Chandler," the inspector asked, not lifting his eyes from the clipboard. "What is the greatest advantage of Artificial Illumination for a factory such as this?"

Chandler's honest answer went up his throat and into his mouth, but it never came out. The truthful answer was that AI was stripping the factory of its soul. The genuine answer was that AI was an evil scheme dreamt by the devil himself to destroy the world. The Antichrist was undoubtedly behind AI, and he was eager to bring about Armageddon. However, the real answer didn't matter and was not allowed to be uttered.

"It provides consistent light," Chandler replied. "I think factories will benefit from AI in several ways and there will be fewer interruptions in work."

"Consistent light," the inspector repeated out loud, writing on his clipboard. "Fewer interruptions..."

"And, of course..." Chandler interrupted, "AI is safer and reduces the risk of fires!"

"Interesting," the inspector said as he stopped writing, "so, you would agree then that AI is safer?"

"Well, yes. But we've always been careful in our factory," he said slowly. "Being careful is what makes things safer in the workplace. The actions of the worker impact safety more than anything else. The same is true for efficiency."

The inspector looked up from his clipboard and he rolled his eyes dramatically. He shot daggers at Chandler, contemplating his next words.

"So," he said, "you believe the burden of safety and efficiency should remain on workers rather than on the system itself?"

Chandler deduced that it was a trick question. He wanted to toe the line between speaking truth to power and not unnecessarily provoking the inspector. He had no idea what consequences could arise should he needlessly offend the man.

"I believe both matter," he suggested. "Skilled workers and reliable systems. AI can reduce accidents and increase productivity, so long as the men using it understand it can never truly replace their hard work and dedication to their craft."

The pen moved again. The inspector didn't smile, but something in his shoulders relaxed. Not far from them, at another workbench that was within hearing range, the second inspector opened a ledger and flicked through its pages. Now and then he made notations beside a number. At one entry he paused, then glanced up, not at Chandler, but at Travis.

Travis, tall and strong, who was typically steady as stone, went rigid. He pretended not to notice the inspector staring at him. He focused on the cooling wax in the molds on his bench, but the tightness in his shoulders and jaw betrayed him. The inspector moved on without comment. Travis did not say a word.

Chandler had interacted with plenty of officials over the years. Men who checked weights at the market or counted crates at the docks were interested in numbers, things you could argue about or bargain over. These men were measuring something else. They were not taking notes about business operations, and they seemed more focused on the staff's personal thoughts and feelings about AI.

The AI fixtures hummed steadily overhead. Their light washed the walls clean of shadows, leaving only thin slivers in the corners and under benches. The old candlelight had left pockets of darkness, creating places a man could stand and think by himself. This new light left no room for self-reflection.

"Remarkable," the second inspector called out, running his fingertips along a drying rack. "There are so many candles in here and so much potential for a hazard."

He wasn't talking to Chandler or anyone from how it looked. His eyes had drifted to the AI lamp mounted above them, as if waiting for it to agree. At the far end of the hall, an apprentice dropped a wick-cutter. The metal clanged against the floor, causing both apprentices to jump. They scrambled to pick it up, moving faster than they would have normally.

"Careful!" the inspector commanded. "Sharp tools and candles don't go together! Situations like this are the reason men like me have a job."

The apprentices looked confused and apologized even though the candles weren't lit. Likewise, handling wick-cutters was not a true hazard, even for the most reckless candlemaker. One apprentice kept saying "I'm sorry, it will never happen again." The other apprentice teared up and begged the inspector for forgiveness like dropping the wick cutter had been personally offensive to him.

The factory had transcended into a state of panic with the inspectors present. Every man kept their eyes low, voices low, and they kept their thoughts to themselves. It was as if thinking negatively about AI was against the rules.

"Do you make it a habit to work beyond your mandated hours, Master Chandler?" the first inspector asked.

"Pardon me?" Chandler pivoted toward him.

"I have a note here that you are often among the first to arrive and the last to leave. Is it a frequent occurrence to disregard your assigned shift?" The man tapped his notes.

"I take my duty to the factory seriously," Chandler stood tall. "Yes, sometimes that means coming early or staying late to make sure orders are met."

The inspector rolled his eyes again. His expressions were a mix of listening, and yet subtly, it was as if he were not paying attention to Chandler's responses at all. It was clear every question was an attempt to bait Chandler into giving a response that could be written down as evidence against him.

"With AI," he admonished Chandler, "such extra efforts will be unnecessary."

"Yeah, I get it!" mumbled Chandler. "AI is the solution to everything." There was a hint of sarcasm in his voice.

The pen came out again as Chandler suspected. He had the urge to snatch the clipboard away, read the notes, and then hit the inspector across the face with it. Part of him wanted to see what was written and the other part of him only desired to fight back. The urge came and went as the second inspector drifted closer. Chandler straightened his posture, picked up a candle he had made the day before, and for no reason wiped it down.

"Someone has been busy," the man observed Chandler's rack of completed candles. "Your output is astonishing."

"Thank you." Chandler agreed, puffing out his chest.

"Your coworkers have adapted so quickly to the reduction orders," the inspector shook his head. "But you, in particular, seem to disregard it, which is not surprising."

"I'm proud of my output," Chandler declared. "I only produce what the inventory sheet directs me to produce. I follow the rules set by my grandfather, Earl Sr., the owner of the Bliss Candle Factory."

The inspector gave a slight nod, but his eyes were already weighing what question he would ask next. It wasn't enough, Chandler realized, to follow the rules. These men didn't care about rules. The men wanted to see how he would respond to being nudged. They wanted to see how he ticked when pushed out of his comfort zone.

The room itself was watching. Men glanced at one another out of the corners of their eyes, not daring to hold anyone's gaze too long. Conversations shrank to fragments. A wrong word in front of these inspectors felt dangerous. The second inspector tipped his head back, studying the rafters stained by years of smoke.

"Old buildings invite sentiment," he said. "Sometimes sentiment slows progress." His eyes dropped back to Chandler. "You understand that, I trust."

Chandler thought of the carved wax horse, the molds in the loft, and the countless stories his grandfather had told over cooling racks at the end of late shifts.

"Yes," Chandler hesitated. "I understand."

Whether he'd just agreed or been issued a warning, he wasn't sure. The inspector moved away again, lips moving as he counted racks. A cold thought settled in Chandler's chest. This inspection was one piece of something already decided. The reduction orders, the promise of compensation, the early installation, none of it felt random. Somewhere there was a file with his name on it. Today's notes would simply be another page added. The first inspector cleared his throat, drawing Chandler's attention.

"Thank you for your cooperation, Master Chandler," the inspector put away his clipboard, and spoke quietly so no one would hear his words. "In times of change, it's important that citizens remain transparent. You are a good man! I am so glad we had a chance to talk!"

What in the Sam Hill was happening? Chandler couldn't tell if the inspector was intentionally trying to provoke him or if he was being kind. Had the last fifteen minutes all been in his head? Had this not been an interrogation disguised as an inspection? Chandler, once again paused, trying to think of what to say next.

"Of course," Chandler replied, trying to be polite. "I am glad we had a chance to speak today. Thank you for coming and have a wonderful rest of your day."

The inspector winked at Chandler and raised his voice so it would carry. He instructed all candlemakers to meet at Chandler's workbench. Without hesitation, the factory, including his family, surrounded him. The inspector was up to something and Chandler became suspicious.

"It appears all candlemakers are complying with the seventy percent reduction orders," he announced. "All but one." His eyes settled on Chandler. "I'm afraid this man's actions have put this week's reimbursement in jeopardy. Unless, of course, Master Chandler here has a good explanation for violating a lawful order."

"Covenant Cathedral, my church, placed a large order that wasn't on the normal inventory list," Chandler explained frantically. "The candles are for services tomorrow. The reduction order must surely exclude places of worship."

"Covenant Cathedral has already been integrated with AI. It was first on the list. You are lying!" the inspector crossed his arms.

"Earl Bliss," the other inspector interjected, turning to the patriarch, "the mayor authorized us to integrate your factory months ahead of schedule, and this is how you repay the favor? Your grandson lies to the Chief Inspector? You might as well spit in Director Vale's face."

Chandler's father apologized at once. Earl Sr.'s expression hardened, gritting his teeth. If he'd been holding a belt, Chandler wasn't sure he would have been spared a beating. His brothers and uncles stared, with anger, shaking their heads. Their rage was written on their faces. They enjoyed the shorter workdays, the easy pay, and the promise of stability. To them, Chandler had endangered all of it.

"A candle sold to a church is still a candle that violates Article Three," the inspector reprimanded Earl Bliss Jr.

"The Covenant Cathedral needs them," Chandler protested.

"Covenant Cathedral does not need candles," the inspector snapped, his hands squeezing his clipboard. "They are fully integrated with AI. Director Vale warned us there might be a detractor here. He failed to mention *he* was also a deviant and a liar."

"I'll comply! I'll comply!" Chandler's face burned. "Going forward, I'll follow the reduction order exactly. Please don't punish anyone here because of my actions. I will ask though, if inspections are to be regular, it would help to have some notice. That way I can..."

"Cook the books?" the inspector interrupted, his voice dripping with contempt.

"That is not what I was going to say," Chandler said through clenched teeth.

"No," the inspector replied. "Of course, it wasn't."

The factory had never felt so quiet even with several dozen coworkers and family members surrounding him. There was only the steady hum of the new lamps filling the air. At last, the inspectors gathered their papers. They left behind a warning for Earl Sr. and a promise to return the following week to "check for progress." Chandler was dismissed early, his pay docked for the entire day. The last words his grandfather said were that he had brought shame upon his family for his actions.

Ashes & Accusations

Chandler sat on the chair by his bed and watched a single candle burn. The flame inside the glass jar trembled as a breeze came through the open window. The candle's flame shared nothing with the sterile light of AI. The candle wavered, it swayed, and it breathed. People didn't sit and stare at candle flames anymore. Not on purpose, anyway.

The time for church service was approaching, but he couldn't bring himself to move. His body was heavy with a tiredness that went deeper than lack of sleep. At night, he tossed and turned in bed. Sleep was replaced with racing thoughts and detailed analysis of everything that had occurred. He rose finally and walked to the window, closing it partway to reduce the draft. The morning light was refreshing. It was a new day, and by the grace of God, would be better than yesterday.

The street outside was strangely quiet for a Sunday. No bright clatter of voices, no clusters of neighbors calling to one another, only the faint ring of distant hooves and wheels rolling across the cobblestones. He turned back toward the candle.

Its warm circle lay across the bedside table, revealing every rough line in the wood. He lowered himself into the chair, elbows on his knees, and he watched the flame lean and straighten, lean, and straighten.

"What are they asking us to give up?" he asked the candle.

The flame said nothing, but its small, steady glow made the room feel less empty. He thought of Earl Sr. at City Hall, nodding along with Director Vale's speech. His eyes had been bright with approval. His grandfather had always been a man of old habits and proud of the family's craft. Seeing him swallow this change so easily felt like watching a great stone pillar agree to be pulverized into sand.

His hand rubbed the side of his face. He couldn't understand how everyone else seemed ready to follow this new light without question. Didn't they feel the same uneasy fear in their chests or the same concern in their hearts? Didn't they fear that something was being taken and wouldn't be returned?

His gaze moved from the candle to his father's Bible on the dresser, which had been given to him at age thirteen. Earl Jr. had always said their work was a calling. Light, he'd told them, was more than earthly. Light brought men closer to God as a reminder of the divine spark. Yesterday, the same man had praised and worshiped fake light.

"Is it me?" Chandler questioned. "Am I the only one who still feels that AI is wrong for humanity?"

Restless, he walked across the room to where his work coat hung on a wooden peg. His fingers brushed the worn sleeves. The glorious scent of wax that once clung to it had faded. Now, it smelled like hot metal and filament. Everything smelled like that since AI had shown up in Hanover.

He marched back to the chair, picked up the candle jar, and raised it until the flame was level with his eyes. Inside, the wick glowed with quiet determination. The flame of the candle stared back at him as if recognizing an old friend.

"People still need you," he told the candle, "even if they forget why they do."

The flame dipped as another draft swept in through the window. Chandler once again went to the window, but this time he closed the latch. A faint but distinct breeze snuck through small cracks at the bottom. The air rushing inside made the candle flicker almost to the point of going out. The wind carried with it something he couldn't name. It was like the world itself was trying to extinguish the flame.

Chandler set the candle down, and he began to get ready for church. He washed in a basin of chilly water, pushed his hair back with grease, and then ironed his nicest shirt. The floor creaked as he moved around. He returned to the candle one last time and blew it out. The flame thinned, then vanished, leaving a twist of smoke curling upward. The smell of warm wax lingered with a sweet aroma.

"Hold fast, my friend," he whispered to the candle.

Setting the jar down, he opened the door. Cool air brushed his face. The sun was no longer shining as gray clouds filled the sky. Outside, a low fog hugged the street, softening the outline of rooftops and blurring the horizon.

Chandler stepped out and pulled the door shut behind him. It was a pleasant enough morning, yet foggier than usual. The walk to Covenant Cathedral wasn't short, but it wasn't long either. He'd completed the same walk thousands of times. Today, the air tasted weird, as there was an ashy edge to it that created a dry sting on the back of his tongue.

As he walked, the fog thickened. It clung to his clothes, crawled into his collar, and turned the world gray. His eyes watered like he'd gotten too close to a bonfire. He slowed down trying to understand what was happening. The smoke was not imagined. It scratched at his throat and his eyes continued to burn.

Footsteps pounded toward him, quick and uneven. Chandler shielded his eyes, trying to see who or what was approaching. A figure burst out of the fog, colliding with him, nearly knocking him to the ground.

"It's gone!" Pike sobbed, throwing his arms around Chandler in a crushing hug. His whole body shook.

Chandler grabbed him by the shoulders and pushed him back. "What's gone? Pike, what do you mean?"

"Master Chandler..." Pike tried to catch his breath as he choked on tears that were streaking down his soot-smudged face. "It's gone, Covenant Cathedral! Burned to the ground!"

For a heartbeat, the street vanished. Chandler heard nothing, saw nothing, felt nothing. He kept replaying the words Pike had just uttered, "It's gone, it's gone, it's gone..." He dropped to his knees, praying out loud, and mumbling to himself.

"No," he pleaded. "No, that's not possible... the Lord's house doesn't burn!" He sprang to his feet as Pike watched him, waiting to see what he would do next.

Chandler didn't wait. His feet moved before he had fully formed a rational thought. He pushed Pike to the side and ran. Ash floated down in slow, gray flakes, clinging to his coat and hair. Each breath filled his lungs with char, causing him to cough uncontrollably.

"Chandler, stop!" Pike chased after him, begging. "You can't go that way! It isn't safe!"

Chandler kept running, disregarding Pike's plea for him to stop. The closer he came to the Cathedral, the heavier the air grew as he choked on debris. Voices rose from somewhere ahead, shouts, sobs, women, and children begging for water. Their cries were muffled by the smoke.

There was only ruin now where the Cathedral had once stood. A heap of debris, ash, and smoldering rubble was all that remained. The great bell tower, which had risen so high it touched the heavens, now lay broken on the street. The blackened tip of the tower was in pieces. The roof of the church had caved in. The charred beams looked like the ribs of a decaying whale.

The stained-glass windows were shattered, and pieces of glass were scattered among the ruins. There were at least ten thousand pieces of brilliant colors, red, blue, orange, purple, and gold shards of the old windows peppered on the cobblestones. Chandler's knees nearly buckled as a crowd had gathered at a wary distance. Some people prayed aloud, others cursed. A few were doing both simultaneously. Everyone held scarves over their mouths and their eyes were bloodshot.

“Not one step closer,” a city guard ordered, blocking Chandler from moving forward. “The heat will melt your skin off!”

“What happened?” Chandler sobbed.

A man beside the guard spat into the ash. He cursed multiple times. “It’s the same damn thing that always happens with candles,” he said bitterly. “One was left burning on the altar, too damn close to the damn curtains.”

“That’s a lie,” Chandler snapped at the stranger. “Pastor Michael was careful with candles. You sir, are out of your damned mind.”

“The only lies I hear are from you, sir,” the man taunted Chandler.

Others in the crowd cheered the strange man and held their fists towards Chandler. A woman spat snot on Chandler, striking him in the face. The masses were eager for anything that sounded like an answer even if the premise of the answer was built on speculation and innuendo. Up until five minutes ago, candles were the only light source, and now they were the Boogeyman hiding under everyone’s bed.

Pike tugged at Chandler’s sleeve and his voice shook with fear. “Master Chandler… maybe Pastor Michael did light a candle. Maybe he did accidentally set it too close to a curtain.”

“No!” Chandler yelled. “He didn’t! The altar was nowhere near any curtains. He has lit ten thousand candles over the last thirty years without any problems."

A woman's voice cut through the noise. It was the same woman who had just spat on Chandler. "That place was a tinderbox!" she cried. "All that nasty old oil and wax. If the church would have used *Artificial Illumination*, this would have never happened."

"It wasn't a candle," Chandler insisted. "Something else did this."

No one was listening to him. Their grief, fear, and anger had already chosen their explanation. A city worker stumbled out of the wreckage, coughing hard. His clothes were streaked with soot. His eyes looked like a cloudy sunset.

"We recovered the body," he called as his voice faltered. "Pastor Michael didn't make it," he wept.

The crowd shuddered as one. Women wailed while most of the men went silent. Everyone alike was stunned. It had only been a week since Pastor Michael and Chandler had chatted after church. The pastor had confided in Chandler that he, too, did not trust AI and wanted nothing to do with it. Now he was gone, dead, already cremated. Pike sank to the ground and covered his face, sobbing, bitterly.

"Where did you find him?" Chandler asked.

"By the altar," the man responded. "It looks like he tried to put the fire out. A small puddle of wax was next to his corpse."

"Candles!" someone shouted. "The ways of old killed him!"

"This wouldn't have happened with AI lights!" another declared.

"Those who resist progress are the problem!" The city worker jumped in, escalating the tension.

Chandler sensed everyone's eyes on him. Everyone knew he carried the last name Bliss, a family known in Hanover for candles. He took a step back, then another, and then another. The tension continued to rise as the volume of the crowds snarled. It was an incredible ruckus.

Pike grabbed his hand. "Don't say anything else," he whispered urgently. "They've already decided what they want to believe."

The crowd kept shouting with fierce anger. The wind picked up, blasting ash across the square, stinging, and blinding their eyes. Chandler blinked hard and used the smoke as cover to escape. He and Pike crept in silence for several blocks until they could no longer hear the crowd. Their shoes scraped through the ash on the ground as they went. The remaining smoke lingered in the air but thinned the further they walked away. They kept their heads down, trying to go unnoticed.

"You made it worse. You shouldn't have provoked them." Pike crossed his arms.

"About what? The pastor?" Chandler asked. "The candles?"

"About anything." Pike kept his voice low. "Not out loud at least, and certainly not with that many people listening."

"Honesty isn't a sin," Chandler quipped.

"In Hanover it is." Pike let out a humorless breath. "Plus, you don't know what happened either."

"You don't believe them, right?" Chandler asked.

Pike opened his mouth, then closed it again. His fingers twitched at his sides. "I don't know what to believe!" he declared. "I saw the fire. I heard the inspectors tell you that the church already had AI installed. I heard you arguing with them." He swallowed. "I know you respected the pastor, but lighting candles is foolish."

Chandler's chest tightened. "You think candles killed him?"

"No! I mean, I don't know what to think. Everyone knows that lighting candles is dangerous and kills..." He trailed off. "Oh, what does it matter what I think?"

"It matters to me," Chandler sighed. "I thought we were on the same side."

"I am on your side." Pike looked away, breaking eye contact with Chandler.

They continued to walk, but slower than before. The silence between them created an empty void. As they neared the industrial quarter, the smoke had thinned almost entirely. Although they had not discussed where they would go, out of habit, they had meandered back toward the factory. Pike and Chandler continued to sob intermittently at the loss of Pastor Michael.

"Whatever happens," Pike broke the silence, "promise me something."

"What?" Chandler glanced over.

"I know you hate AI, but I beg you, please stop picking fights with inspectors and others from Hanover about it," Pike passionately pleaded.

"I can't promise it," Chandler replied.

"I knew you'd say that." Pike's shoulders dropped.

"What do you want from me, Pike?" asked Chandler.

"Did you not see the faces of the crowd back there? They were ready to kill you! I want you to stay alive," Pike cried.

The words Pike spoke, his fear, lodged in Chandler like a splinter. They rounded the last corner of their walk, the brick bulk of the Bliss Candle Factory only a few hundred feet away. Not long ago, there was candlelight streaming from the front windows. Today, heavy dark curtains were hung and bright AI light projected through the cracks. They opened the factory doors to enter.

Inside, Earl Sr. was waiting. That alone was unusual. He never came down on a Sunday unless something serious had happened. His arms were crossed, his face looked like stone, and his eye's radiated fear. Around him stood twenty candlemakers in their Sunday clothes. Some had come straight from the Cathedral as their jackets were sprinkled with ash.

It didn't take long for the shouting to start outside. There were two men at first, banging on the factory doors, demanding to see Earl Sr. Two became four. Four became ten. Shouts multiplied into an off-key enraged chorus. Chandler caught phrases through the crack in the center of the doors.

"Murderers!"

"Curse you all!"

"You burned the Lord's house!"

"You killed a man of God!"

His father and brothers hauled benches and crates to brace the doors. The walls of the factory thudded with each thrown brick.

Chandler opened the corner of a curtain and looked outside. He recognized some of the faces in the mob as they belonged to the demolition crew who had torn down the factory's old fixtures the day before. Now those same men were handing out bricks from buckets, shouting, "The Bliss Candle Factory burned the Cathedral!"

Bricks collided with the walls and windows, shattering the glass. One brick tore through the window Chandler had been peeking through. A shard struck him on the face causing a small cut under his left eye. The sound was like artillery being fired. Inside the factory, they trembled with fear.

The Edict of a New Dawn

The Bliss family, a handful of senior candlemakers, and a few apprentices fled toward the back of the factory, hoping to get out through the rear door. It was no use. When they reached it, they heard men on the other side, shouting insults and blocking the way. The mob's fists pounded on the wood, and they hollered the same exact words as though they had all been provided a script...

"MURDERERS!"

"FIRE STARTERS!"

"CANDLEMAKERS DID THIS!"

"DAMN THEM ALL TO HELL!"

There was no way out and panic rolled through the group. The voices in the factory dropped to frantic whispers. Boots scuffed across the wax-slick floorboards. Two men were holding on to the rear factory doors keeping the mob from coming inside. Someone outside was hammering a piece of wood on the doors trying to break in. The commotion went on for several minutes.

Earl Sr. ordered a few men to loop a thick chain through the rear doors, securing it. He instructed everyone to move to the center of the factory and specifically away from the windows. The pounding on the doors stopped, as if someone had thrown an invisible switch. The only sounds were the ragged breathing of the men inside and the faint hum of the AI lights overhead.

A muffled voice carried into the factory, "Quiet! Quiet now!" Mayor Pembroke yelled from outside the front of the factory.

Another voice joined him. The voice was stronger yet smoother. It was Director Vale commanding silence from the mob. Earl Sr. could be heard thanking God that Vale had come to save them. Chandler and a few others moved cautiously toward the front while most of the men stayed in the center as Earl Sr. had directed. Earl Sr. and Earl Jr. went ahead, marching to the front doors. They unbarred the doors and the mayor's guards pulled them open from outside.

"Good citizens of Hanover," Mayor Pembroke called, standing between the factory and the crowd, hands raised. "This is not the way. Destroying the Bliss Candle Factory is not the way to handle the grief of losing Pastor Michael."

Director Vale stepped forward beside him. His coat was spotless, his silver eye-and-torch pin was polished, and his teeth sparkled. "This is not what Pastor Michael would have wanted," Vale said. "This is not who we are."

“Bliss family,” he shouted toward the open door, “come out here.”

Earl Sr. went first, his shoulders square and his chin held high. Earl Jr. followed, trying to match his father’s confidence. The rest of the family and staff filed out behind them, Chandler among them. Pike followed a few steps behind. The crowd’s insults started again. The words were ugly and harsh, especially from the men Chandler recognized from the demolition crews. They were still holding bricks and cursing the Bliss name.

Earl Sr. ignored them and shook the mayor’s hand. Vale patted him on the back, smiling like they were at a festival instead of standing in front of a riot.

“Gentlemen,” Vale said, turning to face the mob, “the Bliss Candle Factory has embraced AI. They fully integrated yesterday, and they obeyed every order we gave them. Why direct your anger at them?”

“Candles burned the Cathedral!” someone shouted. “A candle killed the pastor!”

Vale spun toward the voice. “Pastor Michael begged me for AI,” he shared. “Churches weren’t scheduled for installation yet, but Pastor Michael came to me insisting. He wanted nothing to do with candles; he hated them. He cared more for the safety of his people than for old habits. Why would you say a candle killed him?”

The crowd stirred and was confused. Some of them seemed relieved and some of them looked more furious. It was hard to understand what they were hoping to accomplish with their protest.

A high-pitched voice cut through the noise, "I know what happened. I know the truth," a woman called.

Chandler's stomach dropped. He knew that voice. She stepped forward. It was the same mysterious woman who had sat watching him at his bench right before questioning him about AI being wonderful. She was the same woman who had greeted the engineers by name when they showed up. She was carrying the same bag with the eye-and-torch emblem.

"That man there," she said, pointing straight at Chandler, "was pressuring Pastor Michael to buy candles after church last week. He badgered him and threatened him. Pastor tried to refuse, but that man threatened to harm his family if he didn't buy more candles."

One of the inspectors from the previous day stepped out of the crowd and stood beside her like he'd been waiting. "Yesterday," he said, "during our review of this factory, that same young man spoke poorly of Artificial Illumination. He told us the Cathedral needed more candles and admitted he would hide future overproduction when we came back."

"He's a scoundrel!" a man roared.

"A no-good varmint!" another bellowed.

"A murderer!" another shouted.

"Cut his head off!" a woman yelled.

Chandler had grown up with some of these people. They were owners of bakeries, and he had bought bread from them. Some of them owned businesses, and he had fixed their candles when wicks burned wrong. A few of them were bankers and Chandler had deposited money with them. Now their faces were full of fury, rage, and a thirst for blood.

Chandler's own family stepped away. His father dropped his hand from Chandler's shoulder as if touching him burned him. His uncles moved away, and one spat on him. Pike loosened his grip on Chandler's sleeve and inched away.

One of Chandler's brothers shoved him to the ground while another kicked him hard in the ribs. The air rushed out of his lungs, and he began a coughing fit. The crowd surged upon him. Shouts rose again, louder than before, demanding justice, for punishment, and a stoning at City Hall's courtyard.

A few men from the mob picked Chandler up from the ground and started pulling him to City Hall. The entire crowd followed. Chandler fell multiple times as they dragged him by his clothes. As they arrived at City Hall, the city guards pulled the mob off Chandler and pushed him to the ground. Then came the sharp blare of a horn. Everyone went silent. From the top steps of City Hall, soldiers drew aside tall red curtains to reveal a raised platform and a podium bearing the silver eye-and-torch emblem.

The soldiers, wearing blue dress uniforms, stood on each side of the podium with their right hands gripping their swords. Director Vale climbed the steps slowly. He placed his hands on the podium and let the silence settle around him. His head shook, showing his disapproval for the situation.

The Edict of a New Dawn - Speech

Good citizens of Hanover. Look at yourselves. This is what fear does. A tragedy strikes, and instead of standing together, you turn on one another. You shout rumors, you slander each other, and you reach for stones. You forget who you are and break all bonds of community.

Pastor Michael believed in God, but equally, he believed in Artificial Illumination. He would frequently tell me there were two divine lights: the eternal and AI. He wanted better light for his people to worship on this side of eternity.

He believed in the future we are building. The Bliss family is not responsible for his death. The Bliss family did not burn his church. Chaos did, carelessness did, and disobedience did. I will not let this city devour itself. We have been given an edict of a new dawn.

From this day forward, anyone who stirs panic, anyone who fights the changes we must make, will answer with the harshest of consequences, I assure you. Progress will not be held hostage by those who cannot embrace it. Go home now and grieve. Don't hope for the death of those who defy AI but pray their souls may be spared from eternal punishment for their sins. Together, we will build a brighter future with AI.

Thank you, God bless you, and God bless Hanover!

Slowly, the mob's roar faded to a mild grumble, then to low muttering, then to nothing. Vale left the podium and came back down the steps. He crossed the square with the mayor at his side and stopped in front of Chandler, who was still on his knees, his face bleeding and bruised.

"Enough," he ordered.

He offered Chandler his gloved hand and pulled him to his feet, patting his shoulder like they were old friends. The mob again yelled, demanding Chandler face consequences for his actions.

"Good citizens of Hanover," Mayor Pembroke called, "this young man's actions will have consequences, but not at your hands."

“Indeed,” Vale agreed. “We will answer tragedy with order, not vigilantism. Out of respect for Pastor Michael and his wish for safer worship, no church, synagogue, or temple in Hanover will be supplied with candles from this day on. Rituals will be performed using AI alone.”

“What about him?” someone shouted, pointing at Chandler. “The boy who pushed the candles on the pastor?”

“As for him,” Vale said, “he will no longer be permitted to attend services at any house of worship in this city.” He altered his voice to mimic a preacher. “God hath spoken! Thou shall not be permitted to worship Him. Amen! And amen!”

The words struck Chandler harder than any stone ever could. He wept, pleading with Director Vale to allow him to go to church. Grabbing at the arm of the mayor, his hands were pushed away. He noticed an odd look in the mayor’s eyes. It was the look of a man who seemed to be feeling regret, worry, and fear.

“The Lord may forgive him,” Vale continued, “but a man who will not trust the light we’ve been given cannot be trusted among those who do. Let that be his punishment. He may look on from outside of the sanctuary and think about his choices.”

Chandler stared at him as blood seeped down his face and stained his shirt. To be turned away from church was worse than death and something he'd never heard done before. Now it was being pronounced on him in the open air. Pike took several steps away from Chandler. Chandler tried to swallow, but there was no moisture in his mouth.

"I didn't kill Pastor Michael," he said hoarsely. "He didn't believe in AI. He despised it."

"How dare you," Vale snapped, all smoothness gone. "How dare you put words in the mouth of a man who can no longer speak? You stand here, after breaking the rules, after working in secret for your own profit, and now you drag a dead pastor into your lies."

He turned, addressing the crowd again. "If true justice existed in the world, this young man's place in his family's business would end today. Perhaps the factory itself should answer for him in flames of its own."

Chandler's father stepped toward him. Slowly, he approached taking small, deliberate steps. His face was flush with shame and fear. He spat at Chandler's feet and slapped him across the face.

"You are no longer my son," Earl Jr. spat again. "You've brought disgrace on us."

His grandfather's voice came next, low but clear. "You are no longer an heir of the Bliss family," Earl Sr. said. "Your name will be struck from every document. You will not inherit a single brick of the factory."

The words hit harder than any blow. All around them, the crowd began to disperse. Stones slipped from hands and fell harmlessly to the ground. Guards waved at those who lingered, giving them direction to move along. People drifted away in small groups, talking under their breath, whispering foul words about Chandler.

Chandler came to his feet. He turned and limped away. No one stopped him and no one cared if he was okay. Pike strutted away with Earl Jr. He took a dozen steps, then glanced back once, glaring at Chandler with contempt.

Mayor Pembroke shook Earl Sr.'s hand. The Bliss family and their workers all went home. Director Vale stood with the demolition men at the edge of the square, handing them money. The same men who had hurled bricks not an hour before now pocketed their pay because they had completed their assigned task.

Chandler pleaded with the Lord, "Please, let this be a nightmare," he prayed. "Let me wake up to wax under my fingernails and the Covenant Cathedral bells ringing for morning service." When he opened his eyes, the faint smell of smoke was still in the air, the AI lights still glared from City Hall, and his grandfather's words still rang in his ears. It was real and he was alone.

Those Who Remain

The day was August 5, 1884. Four months had passed, though time no longer moved the way Chandler remembered it. Days bled into one another faster than a steam engine down the river. Hanover still had mornings and nights, bells, and schedules, but Chandler lived outside of them now.

He slept behind a deli on Ware Street. There was a narrow space between a brick wall and a sagging wooden fence where he lay his head at night. The owners tolerated him because he stayed quiet, because he swept his crumbs, and because he never begged for money. At closing time, the younger clerk would sometimes leave a paper sack containing half a loaf of bread, a small block of cheese, and once, a slice of expired roast beef, which he tucked near the backdoor. Chandler never thanked him directly as showing gratitude had become a dangerous thing in Hanover. It made a man noticeable.

The alley smelled of brine, horse manure, and spoiled vegetables. The only thing that may have smelled worse was the long, unwashed beard growing on Chandler's face. Rats scattered along the fence at night, sometimes coming into his torn blankets. Chandler shared his corner with a stack of broken crates and a discarded sign that once advertised *Free Samples for Customers*. He used it to block the wind. When it rained, water pooled near his boots and soaked his clothes. When it got cold at night, the damp turned into a long, aching punishment.

He had been a master candlemaker once, a man held in high regard. Now he counted his days by scraps and shadows. Hanover was bright now, too bright. Artificial Illumination lined the streets like rows of unblinking eyes. The new lamps hummed faintly, but not loud enough to hear unless one stood still and listened. Chandler listened often, and the sound reminded him of trapped insects that had not accepted their pending death.

People moved differently beneath the lights. They moved faster and rarely did they linger. They did not look at each other anymore. Everyone's face looked aggressive now, stripped of all pleasantness. Candlelight had hidden small flaws. AI was not as kind; it revealed everything.

The first slogans showed up not long after Chandler had been expelled from his family in disgrace. Vale used the Covenant Cathedral fire to justify things that would have been ridiculous before. The slogans appeared on posters, then in shop windows, then painted neatly above doors.

At first, they were optional to recite, then were encouraged as a friendly reminder. Not long after, they were required and enforced with fines. To enter a store, a citizen was asked to repeat the phrase posted above the door. Some shopkeepers did it apologetically, giving grace, reminding shoppers if they forgot. Some shoppers recited the words with pride, as though they had always believed the words. If any customer hesitated for too long, they were asked to leave the store. If they refused, the shopkeeper was required to report it to the Council of Illumination.

Chandler watched it happen from across the street one morning. An older woman, clutching a basket, stood outside the deli. When asked to repeat the slogan, she laughed nervously and said she was too tired. The clerk smiled tightly and shook his head. Within moments, two inspectors appeared as if summoned. They wore dark jackets with blue sleeves, which bore the silver eye-and-torch logo.

They asked the woman her name as part of their *investigation* of a public disturbance. She refused to tell them. She never made it inside the store and Chandler never saw her on that street again. The word *investigated* spread through Hanover. People had learned to fear it more than being arrested.

Updated mandates were issued daily. Following the slogans was the "Moment of Gratitude" rule. When the AI lights turned on each evening, citizens of Hanover were required to stop where they stood, face the nearest lamp, and repeat the phrase "We are thankful for our light" before they were permitted to continue.

The city began printing what was referred to as the *Legacy Citizens List*. The ledger of names was intended to "relieve the strain on shared resources." Those whose years no longer aligned with the city's forward momentum were set to be the last to receive the upgrade or not at all. Families were assured this step in the transition was necessary and dignified, and that no further provisions would be required on their part.

The AI expansion was expensive and required sacrifice. Thus, those unable to contribute to the system forfeited their pensions, and their living spaces were reassigned when necessary. The city spoke of it as balance restored, a necessary easing of weight, and most people accepted the silence that followed as proof the system was working.

Privacy didn't vanish overnight. It was legislated away in increments so small most people didn't feel the loss. First came the removal of shutters, then the ban on heavy curtains, and finally a requirement that every room remain visible from the street so inspectors could confirm "adequate illumination."

Doors had to remain open during certain hours, and households that lingered too long behind them were questioned about "unregistered shadows." Privacy became a suspicious act, a breach of civic duty, a sign that someone might still value darkness for its ancient, forbidden comfort.

Travel within Hanover was also restricted in the name of efficiency, as authorities claimed that uncontrolled movement disrupted AI inspections. To ensure compliance, stability, and implementation, citizens were required to remain where the system could best account for them. Citizens did not always adhere to the mandates, but they were taking a risk when they did not.

Travis Cloud came to see Chandler occasionally. He always arrived at dusk, and he was careful to keep his visits short. He brought bread and butter when he could, sometimes a shirt or socks folded too neatly to have been used. Once, he brought a small tin of wax with a stub for a wick.

"Don't light it," Travis warned. "Just... keep it, my friend."

They would sit for an hour or so, resting on an overturned crate. They kept their voices low. Travis talked about the factory, or at least what remained of it. The Bliss name still hung above the doors, but the work had changed considerably. Candlemakers were not authorized to produce candles. Now they assembled metal housings for AI bulbs. They were taught how to wire buildings for system expansion.

"They don't call us candlemakers anymore," Travis explained. "Your father has reclassified us as AI Techs."

Chandler listened and rarely asked any follow-up questions for it was too painful to hear it all. He had discovered it was safer for his mind to stay only high level on details. On Travis's last visit, he stayed longer than usual. He was not himself that day. He seemed restless and his eyes bounced around in a paranoid fashion. Right before he stood up to leave, he hit Chandler with heavy words.

"They're watching me closely," Travis turned quickly, looking towards the end of the alley. "Not just the government. The people of Hanover, too. None of my conversations are private."

Before he walked away, Chandler mustered the courage to ask about Pike. Travis nodded, trying to find the right words. It was hard for him to say as he knew Chandler and Pike had a close friendship.

"Pike is different now and he speaks like them." Travis lingered. "He asked me about you. Be careful, Chandler. If they come asking, say nothing about me visiting."

Travis left in a flash. He did not come back the next day, or the next day, or the day after that. At first, Chandler assumed he was busy. Then he assumed Travis may be sick. Then he assumed something worse. A week passed, and then another was gone.

Rumors traveled through the city the way smoke once had. Near the entrance to the deli, he heard Travis Cloud was under *investigation*. Then, as he went to beg for bread, he heard Travis had been arrested. Not long after, he was bathing in the river and overheard that Travis had disappeared.

Travis was not the first and he was certainly not the last to face such misfortune. Miss Leslie was investigated and there was a story in the newspaper claiming she had murdered Travis. The accusation was printed on the front page with the caption:

WOMAN ARRESTED FOR THE MURDER OF TRAVIS CLOUD

A dispute over illegal candle smuggling. One woman's act of desperation is a threat to public safety.

Miss Leslie's name appeared once more in a column beneath the headline. There was no trial and she was never seen or heard from again. Chandler knew, though, she was framed. Miss Leslie could barely lift a crate and Travis, a brute, had been twice her size. Truth had become irrelevant in Hanover. AI did not require the truth; it only demanded compliance.

He mourned the loss of his friends, powerless to change it. More people went missing. There was a list of the ones that Chandler knew about. There was a lamplighter, a butcher's apprentice, a baker who had laughed at a slogan, and a seamstress who had accidentally knocked over a newly installed AI lamppost. Each disappearance was explained and each explanation was accepted. The citizens of Hanover learned quickly that belief was easier than resistance.

One night, driven lightheaded by hunger, Chandler made a foolish mistake. As he stood in front of a bakery, eyeing the glazed pastries, a shopkeeper demanded that he repeat the slogan. Chandler opened his mouth and nothing came out. The words refused to come out. The streets were busy with several others trying to get into the shop.

"I forgot how to read," he said.

"Please say it." The shopkeeper's face hardened, not angry, but frustrated.

Chandler shook his head and mumbled “no” under his breath. The humiliation came swiftly as people stared, pointed, and laughed. An inspector wrote his description on a clipboard and asked him to come to City Hall for a *conversation*. Chandler fled into the darkness of the alley. The inspectors followed, but he ducked behind a dumpster.

That same night, someone left a note tucked beneath Chandler’s blanket. The single piece of parchment had no name and no signature.

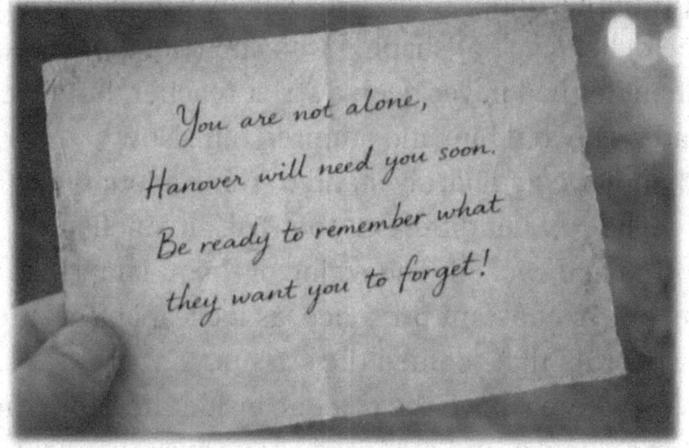

Chandler couldn’t sleep, and he stared at the words until dawn. The alley felt colder. The AI lamps buzzed overhead. The light was dead, but it was patient and eternal. He sat upright, covered in a soiled blanket, as he clutched the small tin of wax Travis had given him. Chandler whispered into the darkness, praying to God for redemption!

The Blueshirts

It was November 21, 1884. The news of Pike's promotion traveled quickly, even to a homeless person like Chandler. Pike had once been a boy, an apprentice under Chandler's steady watch, learning the delicate art of shaping wax and trimming wicks. Chandler had never been a strict teacher, but Pike had respected him and admired him. Now, Chandler could hardly stand to think about him.

The city felt different, too. The air smelled rotten and wicked. The whine of the AI lamps had become a constant presence, as inescapable as the inspectors that roamed the streets. AI was everywhere: above the streets, inside the shops, in homes, banks, and mounted above every window. Hanover was losing not only its warmth, but also its moral compass.

Within a matter of weeks, Pike's face appeared on posters. His portrait was pinned up like he was a hero. The artist had painted his face to make him look more like a full-grown man, and not a fifteen-year-old boy. Beneath his image, there was a large picture of the badge Vale had made for him.

His blue uniform, sewn with buttons plated in gold, sparkled in the sunlight. Daily parades celebrating AI had become the norm. Pike would sit on a float with his shoulders square, his face without blemish, and his hands steady as he passed, waving to citizens. Moreover, the people of Hanover greeted him with reverence like he was their prince. Most people stepped aside and were afraid to make eye contact with him. Director Vale had made Pike the face of the future and the face of Artificial Illumination.

One of Pike's first initiatives was to issue new public safety orders. From the City Hall podium, he issued his first lawful mandate. The Guaranteed Universal Nonviolence Act stated: "Effective immediately, private possession of personal lethal-force devices is no longer compatible with public safety standards and is prohibited within city limits. All citizens must voluntarily turn in such items or have them forcibly removed for the good of all Hanover."

Chandler caught a glimpse of Pike, once, on James Street. Pike was accompanied by two inspectors and a host of armed guards. The mysterious woman, who had questioned Chandler in the factory and accused him of murdering Pastor Michael, was now Pike's personal assistant. She traveled everywhere with Pike, constantly whispering into his ear. He barely saw the people around him and often scoffed at vagrants. Pike's mission was simple… enforce AI implementation and *handle* those who refused.

One morning, the news broke. Chandler's oldest brother had been arrested in connection with Travis's murder. The new official story was that Travis had uncovered an illegal black-market candle trade designed to undermine the AI-powered lighting system. In panic, Miss Leslie and Earl Bliss III had killed him to keep their secret.

The accusation was absurd. Miss Leslie didn't know Chandler's older brother that well. The entire premise was illogical as Earl III had been away attending a University in Boston to study medicine. It was no secret that he could have cared less about the family business. But in a world where logic no longer mattered, where truth could be rewritten with a single stroke of a pen, who was to say what was real anymore? To honor Travis's noble act, Director Vale awarded him the Hanover Medal of Victory posthumously for his willingness to die for AI.

Pike was not named in the news article, but Chandler knew. Pike had a hand in this. The young apprentice that he had taught to mix tallow and trim wicks, now sat in the halls of power. Following the death of his mother in a tragic accident, Pike had gained a reputation for cruelty. In his short tenure as a city official issuing orders, he had become known for his barbarism. It was rumored that he found it humorous to send people like Miss Leslie and his brother, Earl III, to prison forever. He delighted in it.

Pike's *interviews* became the quiet terror of Hanover. Random citizens were summoned one by one into a windowless room lit only by a single candle. Pike never raised his voice and never made threats. Citizens were required to hold their hands several inches above the candle, out of range to be burned, but to feel heat.

Once the citizen felt pain, Pike asked questions about loyalty and progress, smiling as though he were conducting a friendly survey. Depending on the response, the citizen would be required to move his hand closer to the flame. If the person reacted from the burning heat, it was proof he was guilty of treason. If there was no response to the flame touching his skin, it was proof he was an enemy of AI. Regardless of the outcome, the verdict was pre-determined.

The city's streets felt emptier now. There were fewer faces to see and fewer voices to hear. The AI-enforced silence had spread like a disease. People spoke only in hushed tones, repeating the pro-AI slogans under their breath as they passed. Most of them mumbled, but some, who were attending the university, repeated the slogans with a sense of pride.

The next wave of orders came quickly. Pike hired hundreds of inspectors. Most were younger men who had once worked as apprentices in various trades. A good portion of them were students in the university. The younger citizens of Hanover had bought into AI with all their heart, mind, soul, and body. The promise of AI inspired them to enforce the mandate, and it made them feel noble.

To recruit, Pike had fired any teachers in the schools who did not, as he put it, "say with passion and gusto" praises about AI. The inspectors walked the streets with unchecked authority, their eyes like cats, and their ears alert like foxes for any sign of rebellion.

There was gossip that Pike had authorized bounties and offers of compensation for anyone willing to turn in a neighbor or a family member who spoke negatively about AI. Neighbors greeted one another before the workday started, asking vague questions about their AI usage. If the neighbor did not make a compelling enough case regarding his love for AI, then Pike's inspectors would show up to start an *investigation.*

The citizens referred to Pike's young inspectors as "the Blueshirts," and they were terrifying to be around. Every street had its own pair, mostly young men, sometimes women, seated in shadowed doorways. They would hide behind corners, waiting for anyone to slip up and say the wrong thing. The Blueshirts rarely asked questions before arriving at their decision of guilt. When anyone was bold enough to question their tactics, the Blueshirts responded the same way every time, not with anger or pride, but with a generic reply, "We are only following orders."

The first time Chandler encountered a Blueshirt, he froze in place and remained silent. The Blueshirt's eyes locked onto his like a hunting lion stalking its prey.

"Do you believe in AI?" the Blueshirt asked.

Chandler's mind raced, but his mouth refused to move. He shook his head "no," and the Blueshirt stared for a moment longer. If it weren't for another citizen drawing the Blueshirt's attention away from Chandler by refusing to regurgitate an

AI slogan while entering a shop, he would have been taken. He ducked into an alley and ran for several blocks. Chandler learned something that day. The Blueshirts weren't there to listen for dissent. The Blueshirts were there to make sure no one was even thinking about it.

And then came the day when Pike visited Chandler. It was late afternoon, and Chandler sat by the back door of the deli. It was cold and he was wrapped in a blanket that was too thin to make a difference. His hands were wrapped around a small cup of stale broth the butcher's beautiful daughter, Rae, had given him.

Chandler and Rae had grown close over the last several months. He had never meant to fall in love with her. What began as simple kindness had deepened into something he felt in every quiet moment they spent together. In another time, another Hanover untouched by fear, he would have asked for her hand by now. Yet, even as the feeling blossomed, he knew their future together had already been stolen from them.

The street outside was quiet. The hum of the AI lights filled the space between the silence. The buzzing sound in Hanover was constant and grew louder each day. Chandler heard footsteps before he saw the figure. Pike stood behind him. His eyes, once full of warmth, were now empty, cold, calculating, and demonic. His uniform was blue and crisp, with the eye-and-torch emblem prominently displayed on his chest. Vale had awarded him medals for his service which were strung across his left pocket.

Was this Pike? It looked like the guy Chandler had once known. Was this the fifteen-year-old he had taught in the factory? Was this the same boy who had wanted to make his mother proud and had stayed up all night with him making candles before the demonstration? It was him, alright, but it was not him at the same time.

"Chandler," Pike stood at attention, his voice sounded deeper. "I've been looking for you, my friend."

Chandler stood up slowly, his hand gripping the doorframe for support. He took another sip of the broth because he was hungry. The broth was stale but still tasted wonderful on his lips. Rae would always add salt and other herbs to help it taste better, something she did only for him. His eyes glanced at Pike, who was waiting for his reply.

"You were looking for me? What for?" Chandler's eyes met Pike's eyes.

Pike didn't answer at first, but eventually he took a few steps forward. His boots were premium leather, his belt matching the same color and texture. The weight of his boots striking the pavement sounded like he was a massive man, yet his stature was small.

"I'm sorry to hear about Travis," Pike said with confidence, though there was no warmth in his words. "I am glad we found his killers, which must make you happy?"

"Yes, I've heard." Chandler's head tilted.

"Then you know?" Pike shifted his eyes downward. The vagueness of the question was meant to get a response from Chandler. This was the same tactic the Blueshirts used in the streets. Chandler forced himself to look Pike in the eyes.

"Look, if you're here to drag me to some court or investigate me," Chandler jested, his voice dripping with contempt, "arrest me and be done with it."

"I'm not here to arrest you," Pike scoffed. "I only came to talk to you."

The two Blueshirts that accompanied Pike were watching to make sure Chandler did not do anything stupid. He had barely moved and already the two enforcers looked like they were ready to jump him. Chandler had heard the "I just want to talk" routine from others who wore the badge of authority, those who held power to make people comply. Pike realized that Chandler was not going to take the bait, so he started speaking again, though, this time, he tried a different tactic.

"They're going to come for *us* if we don't comply. The old ways... everything *we* stood for, Chandler." Pike's words were measured, spoken with arrogance, and carefully chosen. “You don’t want to be on the wrong side of history. I thought you understood that already.”

Chandler took a slow breath, his mind racing. Pike was using phrases like *we* and *us*, but there were problems with these statements. Pike had become the enforcer, the one who would keep everyone in line. He had become what Chandler had always feared, a man who had traded his soul to gain the world. Likewise, Pike had used the word *stood.*

“I never wanted any part of this,” Chandler raised his voice. “You can’t twist things like this, Pike. You can’t rewrite history. You have changed; you are no longer an honorable man!”

For the first time since the conversation began, Pike’s expression faltered and his voice sounded sincere. It was subtle, nothing more than a brief hesitation, but a clear flicker of doubt appeared in his eyes.

“You think I have a choice?” Pike responded. “You think you have a choice?” He laughed. “None of us do!”

The Blueshirts, both college-aged men, looked at young Pike, anger burning in their eyes. Chandler opened his mouth to argue with Pike, but the words died before they could take shape. Pike stomped away like a bitter child. The Blueshirts followed their leader, but Chandler could see a seed of doubt taking root in them. Before Pike reached the end of the alley, he stopped and yelled at Chandler.

"You don't have to fight this, Chandler," Pike declared. "I can give you back your old life, your house, tasty food, you name it… I can give it all back by the end of the day."

Chandler didn't answer. He stood still until Pike walked away, the sound of his footsteps fading into the distance. The words Pike spoke hung in the air long after Pike had gone. What did he mean he didn't have a choice? He thought about the proposal Pike had made. His thoughts drifted as he considered sitting with his family at his grandfather's table, laying in his old bed, and no longer digging through garbage bins for his next meal.

Chandler caught sight of his reflection in an AI light fixture. His clothes were torn; his beard was rugged and unkempt. There was no going back. He eventually fell asleep. In the morning, he heard that Rae had disappeared in the night. The Blueshirts wrote the report that she had run away, never to be seen or heard from again.

Chandler cried for days, weeping bitter tears. He placed a trembling hand to his mouth, trying to breathe. Memories of their time together flooded his mind, her smile, her touch, and the taste of her lips. The grief came in waves, crushing him. The one person who proved he was still capable of love had been taken. Hanover felt colder than it ever had before, as if her absence had extinguished whatever faint, stubborn light remained in his heart. He didn't know it yet, but the world was preparing to take even more.

Where The River Bends

Earl Bliss Sr. died on a Tuesday and that alone felt wrong. Important men were not meant to die on ordinary days. They only passed away on Sundays, after church, or on the battlefield after performing a noble deed. Earl Bliss Sr., patriarch of the Bliss Candle Factory, the single most important man in Chandler's life, died on a Tuesday, having fallen down the stairs in the factory.

Word on the street was he hadn't died instantly from the fall. He suffered in the hospital, for hours, alone, before succumbing to his injuries. Because the Blueshirts had erected a permanent checkpoint at the hospital's entrance, it was challenging for anyone to get in. Chandler was crushed. Grief was not a strong enough word to describe how he felt. This was anguish, sorrow, and agony of the purest form.

The announcement of his grandfather's death came several days later in a single-column on page three of the *Hanover Journal*, wedged between updates about the James Street expansion and a civic reminder about AI slogan compliance.

The front page of the paper was written by a professor claiming that by 1939, the excess heat put off from products requiring combustion would cause irreversible damage to the planet. The professor claimed that Organic Illumination would cause wars and famines. Page two was an article diving into the fact that apprenticeships, which factories relied on for staffing, were a form of systemic oppression.

Chandler flipped back to the tiny blurb regarding his grandfather's passing. No cause of death was listed and there was no obituary. The newspaper listed a name, a date, and a short line about Earl Sr. being "a champion of change who was dedicated to progress." Chandler read the article three times before he believed he was not in a nightmare.

Chandler stood warily across the street from Covenant Cathedral on the day of the funeral. The newly built Covenant Cathedral was an industrial-style building. There was no tower, no beautifully colored window panes, no crosses, and no ringing bell. AI lamps lined the entrance, their white glow making the building look sterile and nothing resembling a house of God. The doors were open, but the Blueshirts blocked the entrance, checking pins, checking hands, and checking loyalty.

Chandler did not have the required emblem, though he did consider stealing one to attend the funeral, but he was no thief. Inside, he could see movement through small windows. A children's choir sang the song "This little light of mine, I'm gonna let it shine, let it shine, let it shine, let it shine." At the end of the song, the new pastor, Delores, from the west coast, asked the children what light they would let shine. The children, and some of the adults, responded with "AI, amen."

All the men inside wore black coats and polished shoes. They bowed their heads for a moment of silence. Chandler saw his father, standing rigid near the front. Earl Jr. did not look like he had been crying. He gave head nods and half-cocked smiles to Director Vale who looked like he was preparing to give a eulogy. Pike stood near the front, on the left side of the aisle. He looked immaculate in his uniform and put his hand over his heart, pretending to mourn, when people looked at him.

Chandler watched them carry the coffin out. It looked smaller than a normal coffin, like it was made for a child. The coffin was polished black and bore the gold-plated eye-and-torch logo. The man who once commanded a factory, a titan of industry, was now only a shrunken memory, laid to rest in a small box.

When the funeral was over and the crowd dispersed, his brothers, uncles, and aunts, walked towards him, but they looked straight ahead like he had never existed. That night, Chandler wandered the streets until the lamps flickered on. He didn't have a destination or care about where he walked, he just walked. The city blurred around him, shapeless and distant. Hanover no longer smelled like wax and bread. It smelled like metal, damp stones, and death.

A block from City Hall, someone touched him on the shoulder and placed something into his hand. Chandler tried to get a good look at the man's face, but he did not recognize him.

"Don't stop walking," the man instructed.

Chandler didn't stop but glanced back as the man turned right onto the next street. Chandler walked for another two blocks, turned left, and walked a few more blocks. He was terrified to look at the paper the man had slipped into his palm. It was a folded scrap of parchment, thin and worn.

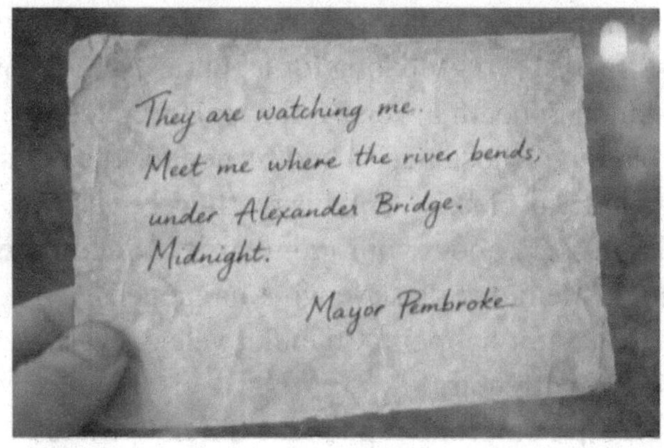
They are watching me.
Meet me where the river bends,
under Alexander Bridge.
Midnight.
Mayor Pembroke

At the bottom of the message, it was signed, "Mayor Pembroke." Chandler laughed. He wondered if he had hallucinated the whole thing because he had not eaten or slept in days. He asked a local vendor if the paper he was holding was real, being careful to hide the message. The vendor replied "Yes" and walked away in a hurry.

Chandler went to Alexander Bridge at midnight as instructed. The river was lower than it had been earlier in the year. Vale had diverted most of the water for the power plant to use. "Where the river bends" referred to a small area under the bridge known for criminal activity. The AI lights glared down from above, but the underside of the bridge was in the shadows. Chandler arrived early and waited, heart pounding in his chest. His heart was filled with a fear he hadn't felt since the first slogans appeared.

Pembroke came alone, dressed in plain clothes. His gray hair was too long for a politician, most of it hidden beneath a worn-out cap. He looked like an old man whose health had turned for the worst. His face was blotchy, and his teeth were yellow.

"I'm sorry about your grandfather," Pembroke stated. "He didn't deserve what happened."

"You let it happen!" Chandler yelled, eyes swelling with tears.

"Yes," Pembroke replied, he did not protest.

Chandler fell to his knees and wept. Throughout the funeral, he had kept it together, but now his tears flowed uncontrollably.

"Vale has seized all control!" Pembroke said, as he put his hand on Chandler's shoulder. Chandler, still crying, shrugged away. "The Council of Illumination. Pike's promotion. The Blueshirts. The courts. He even controls the journalists at the newspaper. I swear, Chandler, I thought I could manage him, but I was wrong. He won't stop!"

"You sold the city!" Chandler shouted, jumping to his feet.

"I thought I was saving it. I thought AI would serve our great city," Pembroke replied, raising his voice. "AI made sense to me. On paper it made sense, efficiency gains, increased productivity, and improved safety. It still makes sense, but it doesn't serve us anymore."

"It never served us," Chandler laughed bitterly.

"He is not done; he is planning more," Pembroke added. "Candlemakers, blacksmiths, bakers, lamplighters, anyone connected to products that use flames. There is no place for people like you anymore."

"Trust me, I know," Chandler asserted. "We don't work with AI now; we work for it!"

"There's talk of new mandates that are stricter and will make it illegal to make anything requiring an open flame. The mandates target candlemakers." Pembroke nodded grimly.

"And if people refuse?" asked Chandler.

"Criminal charges, disappearances, forced confessions, or worse. You don't know what Pike can do," Pembroke swallowed. "I'm not safe anymore either. Vale doesn't need or want a mayor."

Chandler and Mayor Pembroke stood shoulder to shoulder like conspirators, which in truth, they were. Although neither of them had said it, they both were thinking... sedition.

"There's a central source," Pembroke whispered. "It's centralized and hidden. It is highly protected, but vulnerable. AI depends on it to survive. Without it... the lights go out."

"You want me to destroy it?" Chandler looked at the river, the AI lamps reflected off the surface.

"I want you to help me end this. You are the only one I trust," Pembroke replied and he walked away into the night.

By early the next morning, Vale's propaganda machine reached new heights of absurdity. The posters appeared overnight, written in bold letters and hung on every street post. In addition, couriers were sent to every business owner informing them of the new slogans.

The paper ran stories every day about candlemakers being part of a cult. They made claims of secret satanic rituals performed after hours at the Bliss Candle Factory. An article accused the factory of being funded by foreign countries. One specific editorialist didn't outright say it, speaking only in innuendo, but there was a heavy inference that Earl Jr. and other leaders at the factory had conspired to kill Earl Sr.

There were new editorials every day. They explained that small disruptions in AI lighting were acts of "sabotage from the deplorables in the factories." People spat on and insulted anyone who was associated with products that used a flame.

To bring unity and peace, Vale ordered that all tradesmen be temporarily reassigned to factories assembling only AI components. He had traditional workshops boarded up to prevent acts of vandalism.

On Wednesday, he gave an impassioned speech at City Hall calling for all of Hanover to cease violence and to live in harmony. Near the end of his speech, Vale made several comments about losing his patience with those who promoted Organic Illumination and referred to them as "bitter-clingers to tradition that must be *discontinued.*"

Chandler walked to one of the new AI factories and watched from the street. The men he'd known his entire life were present. They lined up outside their new factory assignments, beneath white lights, their heads bowed, wrists stamped with the eye-and-torch. Their hands were still working but no longer did they shape anything of their own. They did not talk to each other nor were there any smiles or small talk. When they left for the day, they looked broken.

With AI lights, the pubs stayed open all night, and that is where most of them found comfort. The bottle made them feel warmth. Chandler could empathize as he, too, had found mercy in a bottle, but it didn't last long enough, and his gut began to rot. The men would drink all night, reflecting on all they had lost. They no longer worked with light in their hearts for the light had left them.

That night, Chandler went back to his bed near the deli. He lit the candle he had kept hidden all these years. It was the same candle he had lit at his mother's funeral when he was a boy. The flame trembled at first but then proudly held the flame. It was in that fragile glow that he understood what he needed to do. Something stirred in Chandler. It was a fire, but not the kind that came from a candle.

War Has Already Begun

The world was nothing more than a machine now. Its gears turned with a relentless and menacing mechanical grind. Hanover's streets shimmered beneath the unforgiving light of the AI lamps, their sharp white light cut through the city like a medieval dagger. There was no longer a flicker of warmth in the city's soul. The last traces of candlelight were disappearing, fading from shop windows, from homes, from faces.

Even in the quiet and most remote corners of the city, the hum of AI never stopped. The city never slept. People learned to speak faster, think faster, and act faster. The city and citizens alike had adapted and evolved, as they always did. But this evolution wore a mask of pretend cheerfulness. Vale had declared 1884 as the golden year for Hanover, but beneath the surface, fear, anxiety, and lawlessness ruled.

Citizens moved through their days with efficiency, as promised by AI. The people's faces were now more like blank slates, eyes straight ahead, bodies moving with a purpose. Everyone's mind was consumed with the next task. New mandates were put in place stating that after nightfall, it was illegal for citizens to converse in natural light, including that of the moon. All interactions, by regulation, had to take place under artificial illumination.

Blueshirts were everywhere as their ranks reached a thousand. Not all were equally committed to AI as some simply wanted to fit in. The most zealous of the Blueshirts remained perched on rooftops, lingering on all street corners, and standing inside businesses. They didn't pretend to shop or give a reason to be there. They didn't speak to anyone as there was no need. Their presence alone was enough to silence dissent and to remind everyone of The New World Order.

The Blueshirts, at the direction of Pike, had adopted a motto they repeated to each other as a greeting. When passing on the street, they would call out "Ordo Orbis Terrarum!" (New World Order) The other Blueshirts, within earshot, responded with "Ordo Orbis Terrarum!" While it brought unity to the Blueshirts, the catchphrase was also meant to intimidate anyone nearby.

Still, a few stubborn voices persisted, even with the menacing presence of the Blueshirts. Occasionally, Chandler noticed them in the streets. The resistance had started quietly. With every disappearance of one person, the resistance grew by two. The numbers grew slowly, with whispers in alleys, and sometimes as little as a facial expression toward another citizen. There were people who refused to wear the emblem and refused to comply with reading the slogans above the doors.

Blacksmiths, candlemakers, lamplighters, bakers, those who had been pushed aside by AI, now found solace in one another's company. Deep down none of them felt genuine hope that their efforts made a difference. Pike, once the boy Chandler had mentored, was now Hanover's greatest threat. Chandler had seen him personally patrol the streets more than once. Other Blueshirts, although unpleasant, would occasionally show signs of some human decency.

Not Pike, though. His eyes were cold as slate. On one occasion, a homeless man told him bread and milk were no longer affordable. In response, Pike laughed, dismissing him, as though poverty were an inconvenience to be mocked. Vale's prince of AI loved to harm others, specifically the older citizens of Hanover. He would go from house to house, business to business, and church to church. Accosting citizens had less to do with AI and more to do with absolute power and domination.

And yet, Pike didn't seem happy. Chandler had occasionally come across Pike in the streets. Much to Chandler's surprise, it was like Pike didn't remember their conversation outside of the deli.

Sometimes, Pike greeted Chandler with pleasantries and other times, he scowled and mumbled cruel words under his breath. It was as if there were two Pikes in the same body.

One thing was for sure, Pike hadn't found peace in his new role. He moved like a man with no purpose in life. His eyes appeared to be possessed by a legion of demons. He babbled incoherent sentences in tongues and required his Blueshirts to do the same. On Sundays, Pike went to church at Covenant Cathedral, but all mentions of Christ were scrubbed from the sermons.

Pastor Delores gave feel-good messages and frequently mentioned how grateful the congregation was for Vale and Pike. She claimed God had told her that "AI deserved to be worshipped." The AI *Sacrament* was introduced as a form of purification. During church services, citizens gathered around an AI light, its white glare so intense it nearly consumed every face.

One by one, people stepped into the circle of heat, lifting their chins as instructed so the light could "search them for shadows." The deacons decided whether the person was worthy of receiving the sacrament. For a small fee, citizens could buy indulgences for any sins they may have committed against AI.

The deacons held *gatherings* where excess, indulgence, and moral abandonment were encouraged as forms of expression. Acts once universally condemned were normalized, first behind closed doors, and eventually in public, in a way that reminded many of the biblical warnings of Gomorrah.

Delores was promoted from pastor to the role of bishop. She began staging miracles for the crowds, each one more shameless than the last. She stood outside Covenant Cathedral in front of a table that held lit candles, arms raised as if pulling power from heaven. At the command of her voice, Blueshirts, disguised as normal citizens, would inconspicuously extinguish the candles with concealed pumps. Simultaneously, AI lights would turn on as the candles went out. She proclaimed that Artificial Illumination had "conquered the flame."

When a woman in the front row collapsed from hunger, Delores healed her. Of course, she never mentioned the stimulant Pike had slipped the woman minutes before. She even paraded a blind man onstage, announcing that AI had restored his sight, though everyone who knew the man understood he had never been blind. Yet the indoctrinated gasped, wept, and fell to their knees, eager to believe the miracles. Pike clapped and shouted "hallelujah!" Even though he was in on the scam, he still appeared to be amazed by the outcome.

Chandler did not fully understand what had happened to Pike. He thought back to Pike's comments outside of the deli. Was Pike trapped, too? Did he truly not have a choice but to pursue such an evil path? Was anything Pike did authentic or was he a puppet? Perhaps Vale's tyranny had swallowed him whole, as it had swallowed the rest of Hanover.

With all of Pike's depravity, Chandler took heart that redemption for his old friend may still be possible. Chandler prayed several times for Pike's repentance that he would turn from his evil ways. All hope was lost, however, when Chandler heard new rumors of a program spreading throughout Hanover. Pike had written the program and launched it himself. The program was terrifying to think about and was straight from the pits of hell.

The program was called **Children for AI**. The release of the program was announced during the Easter service at Covenant Cathedral. Chandler's blood ran cold as horrifying images formed in his mind. Children, the future of Hanover, were being conditioned to pledge loyalty to AI. They were taught to report their parents, their neighbors, anyone who dared question The New World Order. Children, once their parents' greatest asset, were now puppets for the government.

The program was intertwined into all curriculum in the schools, including science, mathematics, and English. Some schools required older students to publicly recite the pledge to AI before being awarded their diplomas. All students were required to wear the eye-and-torch pin on their school uniforms. If they didn't, they would be outcasts. It was the perfect plan. To control the students, was to control the parents. If you dominated the schools, the rest would follow.

City-run orphanages taught harmless rhymes meant to help little ones remember their "light safety obligations." Precious voices drifted from open windows. Their voices were bright and cheerful as they chanted the lines in perfect unison: "*The Devil lives in the dark, he waits for your spark. Keep the light bright, or he comes in the night.*"

The nuns, both in the orphanage and in the parishes, applauded the youngsters' enthusiasm. Children repeated the rhyme at bedtime as though it were scripture. And soon every child in Hanover knew the words by heart, humming them under their breath whenever a bulb flickered. The city had found a way to weaponize fear, planting it early, shaping young minds to tremble at the mere idea of nightfall.

Outside of schoolyards, Pike hosted massive parties, burning books that taught anything seen as traditional. The children were given desserts and sweet drinks. They danced around, tossing books into the massive bins of fire. Literature, Bibles, biographies, and textbooks that taught the history of Hanover were burned.

The most monstrous element of Pike's new program was a rumored initiative referred to in whispers as the "Reduction of the Non-AI Compliant." Chandler could never confirm it, nor did he know anyone who would admit to witnessing it directly, but procreation rights were said to be quietly regulated from City Hall.

Children born to known AI dissidents were flagged, and some were taken from their homes, their names no longer spoken aloud. Everywhere there were forced smiles, but behind closed doors, there was weeping and gnashing of teeth.

Chandler walked the streets that night, his eyes searching for anything to bring him comfort. Was there anything in Hanover that still held to tradition? No, the world had changed. The street lamps stood like sentinels, their artificial light harsh and unyielding, blinding with perfect light.

Everywhere he looked, he saw the insignia: the eye and torch. It was tattooed into skin, sewn into the seams of uniforms, and graffitied onto the sides of buildings. The founding fathers of Hanover had established the crest at City Hall: the Eagle with a serpent in its mouth. That, too, was replaced. The eye-and-torch had become Hanover's new seal. The logo represented submission, control, and the erasure of everything they had once known. Below the crest were the words "Ordo Orbis Terrarum!"

The newspapers reported dozens of arrests daily. The disappearances increased, as well. The Blueshirts referred to the disappearances as *evaporations*. Accusations of "sabotage" against those who had refused to embrace AI were tossed around in the streets, schools, and businesses.

Chandler couldn't stay silent. He had always known that AI had come to claim what was theirs, what his family had built. But now, it was taking everything, their homes, their jobs, their future. It was taking their children by force and demanding their souls in return. The resistance had been small and scattered but not anymore. The anger that had burned quietly inside Chandler for almost a year now had a voice. The fire of defiance was still alive.

The first step in resisting was simple enough. He needed to gather those who had been left behind by AI. People who still loved the old world, such as the old candlemakers, lamplighters, smiths, and shopkeepers who refused to comply. They met in secret, and their numbers grew slowly. They spoke in innuendo and code only, talking about severing what fed the lights.

The plan was reckless, dangerous, and had little chance of working. It would mean destroying the thing that had kept the AI system alive, but it also marked them for certain death. If the foundation of the AI machine that had consumed them all was this unholy thing, then there was only one tactical step possible. The cost would be high, however, and it would mean fighting back in ways they had never dared before.

Chandler knew if they didn't act soon, there would be nothing left to save. As Chandler stood beneath the AI lamps that night, meeting with his comrades, always watching for Blueshirts, a chilling thought gripped him. If the source of what fed the lights was destroyed, would it make a difference? Was AI inevitable?

AI didn't care about history or tradition. It was lifeless, not caring about what had come before. It only cared about what was next and what would make it more powerful and permanent. Chandler couldn't articulate his concerns, and he feared trying to explain his internal struggle with AI ultimately winning would deflate the courage of the others. One thing was for sure; the war had already begun.

PART III

"The Light Beneath The City"

Blame the Flame

There was a fire on Monday. It started in a small warehouse on the south side of Hanover, the last part of town converted to Artificial Illumination. The authorities called it an accident, faulty wiring, no ongoing risk to the public. The installers were overworked and the circuits were overpowered. It was simply a "rare malfunction." The flames tore through the building before dawn, filling the sky with black smoke.

By the next morning, the narrative had already been rewritten. Vale released a polished statement from City Hall referring to the fire. It read, **FLAME-BASED SABOTAGE SUSPECTED**. At noon, he gave a speech from outside the smoldering warehouse stating that "the perpetrators would be punished to the fullest extent of the law." Vale pounded his fist on the wood and communicated with passion. He spoke about peace, love, and vengeance in the same sentence.

Chandler stood at a distance among the onlookers. He kept his coat pulled tight around him, covering his face, and watching the ruins. The original newspaper article stated there had been no candles, oils, or wax in the factory that burned. A retraction was printed several hours later stating that all three were found at the scene.

All Chandler could see was twisted metal and scorched wire. He also detected the unmistakable smell of burning insulation. Still, the crowd spread rumors about candlemakers sneaking in and lighting lanterns during the night. The crowd was not there by accident because Pike had assembled a mob of young activists from the university. They had been trained well.

"Damn candlemakers!" a student shouted.

"How much longer will this chaos be allowed to continue?" a professor taunted.

"Figures they would do this," another added. "They will pay for this!"

The second fire came two nights later. Then, another a few nights after that. The fires were small at first, shops, storage rooms, and closets. Each had been wired hastily for AI by installers who lacked experience. People at the scene when the fires started all said the same thing. "The lights flickered for a few minutes, there were sparks, and then the lights went out before the flames started."

The power feeding the area went out, plunging whole blocks into darkness so suddenly it made people panic. Without candlelight or lanterns, there was nothing for people to rely on. People ran blindly down the streets, trampling one another. The children cried until they were hoarse. Criminals took advantage of the AI failures, using the darkness as an opportunity for unspeakable evil.

When AI went out, all factory work came to a standstill. Workers waited for instructions from their leaders that never came. The leaders had no clue how to operate without AI. They had forgotten all critical thinking skills required to operate without it. Food sat in crates for days and entire shipments spoiled. Widows and orphans starved, waiting for their next meal. AI, the great promise of efficiency, was suddenly the killer of productivity. And still, the blame shifted to those who desired to preserve traditions.

Pike, in his fury, ordered the old posters be ripped down and new posters mounted overnight.

The *Hanover Journal* ran editorials accusing pro "Organic Illumination" hacks of staging attacks to undermine progress. The articles claimed several anonymous sources had provided evidence of their malicious deeds. Yet no one was specifically named in the article as the perpetrators. Everyone understood who was being blamed.

Those who had been candlemakers were taken from their homes in the middle of the night. They were dragged into City Hall for questioning. Old men with burned hands and stiff joints were interrogated under white lamps buzzing angrily overhead. If they didn't confess to being part of the conspiracy against AI, they disappeared. Pre-written confessions were placed in front of them. Sometimes *motivation* was used to force them to sign.

Chandler heard rumors of what was happening, but he was never chosen by Pike or the Blueshirts for questioning. Part of him wondered why Pike had not targeted him. He speculated that since he was not first, he may be the last to be pulled in for questioning. In the few times he had seen Pike over the last several weeks, there was something off in the way he smiled at him.

Entire neighborhoods were sealed off. Blueshirts, lacking a warrant, were granted authority to enter homes without notice. Candles, any and all candles, were confiscated on sight. A couple was beaten in front of their family for keeping their wedding unity candle discreetly tucked in a drawer. A birthday party was staked out and raided for having a candle on the cake.

Blueshirts organized what was framed as "community cleansings," cheerful gatherings where citizens were encouraged and expected to surrender the relics of the old world. Officials smiled as they fed the flames, praising the crowd for their patriotism. The fire was not meant to destroy objects, it was meant to cauterize the past.

The smell of the city changed again. Smoke from the power plant saturated the air. It was not the gentle residue of tallow or sweet smell of lavender. The smoke was thick, causing people to choke on the fumes. Everyone's eyes were bloodshot, and the rain burned with acid. When AI went out, the sewage system failed, and waste backed up into the streets.

The river filled with toxic runoff, killing all the wildlife. Factories that produced AI components dumped chemicals without restraint. Hanover had begun selling AI parts to other cities and their expected output quotas from Vale were beyond measure. Vale had seized all means of production, claiming that private industry was an enemy to progress. He gave elaborate speeches on giving power back to the people through government intervention.

Crime went through the roof, driven by hunger and desperation. Armed robbery, shoplifting, and pickpocketing were among the most common of offenses. People stopped going out at night, not because of darkness, but from fear of their fellow citizens.

Fights broke out on every corner when people refused to give up their wallets to thieves and robberies turned violent if there was any hesitation from the victim. The Blueshirts looked the other way unless a slogan was violated. They didn't care and sometimes encouraged it.

Chandler walked past a burned storefront and saw the words rebels had painted across the brick:

The next day, the Bliss Candle Factory burned to the ground. It happened right before dusk. Chandler smelled the smoke before he saw it. There was a scent of wax, smoke, and something else he couldn't name. Chandler grieved as his past died.

The flames roared through the old building, devouring the beams that had held the Bliss family in a place of honor for generations. Chandler arrived quickly, running to the factory. He witnessed the remaining AI lights in the factory popping with sparks. Men in city uniforms attempted to fight the fire. They arrived late and worked half-heartedly, some of them joked as they pretended to fan the flames instead of extinguishing them.

The mob gathered outside of the rubble. Chandler pushed and clawed his way through the masses, his heart pounding. Bodies were being pulled from the debris. He recognized his uncles and a few of his cousins. Several of the dead were men who Chandler had as apprentices over the years. One of the older men had been his mentor. Most of the remains were charred beyond recognition, their features erased by the flames.

The fire burned hot and fast, as if kerosene or an accelerant had been used. The next morning, the *Hanover Journal* printed the following:

HANOVER JOURNAL

FLAMES AT THE BLISS CANDLE FACTORY SHOCK THE TOWN

Citizens Demand Swift Reckoning

EARL BLISS JR. RESPONSIBLE FOR FACTORY FIRE
CANDLES IGNITE TRAGEDY
JUSTICE TO BE DEALT QUICKLY

The article claimed Earl Bliss Jr., the son of Earl Sr., and the acting leader of the Bliss Candle Factory, had been careless. He'd intentionally used a candle near kerosene to prove that candles were not dangerous. The article highlighted poor leadership and the arrogance of the old ways of living were to blame. Chandler read the words until he was actively weeping.

People passing down the street, also reading the paper, nodded as they carried on with their day. They agreed the article made sense and they had always known Earl Jr. was a scoundrel. Many of them intertwined bursts of profanity into their remarks when mentioning the Bliss family. It was easier to believe the paper than to question or to use their own brain to think. It was easier to blame the past than to embrace the obvious failures of AI.

Chandler stood at the edge of the factory ruins that night. The crowd had gone. Everything that the Bliss family had stood for was destroyed. His father had not been seen since the fire happened. People assumed he had fled Hanover before he could be arrested.

The AI lamps on a nearby factory hummed in the distance. The lights flickered on and off, showing an occasional spark from the wires. No one was willing to admit it, but for the first time, people were afraid of AI. Hanover chose to believe lies and the consequences had proven deadly.

Hanover Eats Itself

The resistance did not announce itself. There were no mass gatherings, slogan chants, or pledges of allegiance. No one wore pins or symbols identifying their loyalty to Organic Illumination. The resistance took shape the same way termites infest a home, quietly, beneath the surface, and in places no one thinks to look. Chandler never desired to lead it, but people simply started searching for him.

They came at night, alone or in pairs. They knocked on the doors of abandoned shops, slipping notes to each other, and stalking alleyways trying to find him. The resistors of AI were former candlemakers, lamplighters, tailors, bakers, smiths, cobblers, and more. They were people who had lost jobs, homes, sons, daughters, and their faith, people who had watched their neighbors disappear and decided they couldn't live in fear any longer.

They did not ask Chandler to give eloquent speeches from podiums. All they wanted was to ask him questions. *What do we do? How do we stop this? How do we survive another day in Hanover?*

Chandler had no grand or fantastical answers. What he had was the memory of Hanover before AI. He remembered the generational lessons he learned from his grandfather.

Even the best systems were fragile, and the strongest leaders were susceptible to failure. The years of hard work in the factory and the countless hours of experience as a candlemaker had taught him many valuable lessons. He recalled how life was when it depended on steady hands and patience. He remembered how the city felt before it forgot itself.

Thankfully, that was enough to lead the resistance. They met beneath bridges and in boarded-up factory rooms. Candles were forbidden and considered contraband by the Blueshirts, so they worked in darkness or by the faint glow of AI. Every meeting carried risk, and every new face could potentially be a spy from Vale.

Every night, the number grew by the dozens. Pike knew about the resistance, as his personal assistant had coached him to expect it. Vale, at The Department of Industrial Development, noticed, too. The *unburdening* orders for Chandler came that day. The orders were not written and distributed as other previous mandates had been. These were different. Blueshirts were allowed to *unburden* anyone they *felt* was associated with OI if they documented the occurrence.

Chandler was never mentioned by name, as the Blueshirts roamed the streets demanding citizens share information about the location of their leader. Chandler's name was not mentioned because everyone knew who they were seeking. Pike was the man who authorized the order to eliminate Chandler. He told himself it was necessary. Disorder had to be cut out before it spread, and he reasoned that OI would sabotage hospitals, schools, and children's programs.

Pike told himself Chandler had become dangerous to the greater good, and it was the only solution to ensure The New World Order was not threatened. Without admitting it to himself, Pike remembered Chandler's friendship, his patience, kindness, humility, and compassion.

Blueshirts covered more ground than they ever had, moving faster. Up and down the block, doors were kicked in and homes searched without warrants. Suspects were taken into custody for questioning, screaming and yelling they were pro-AI, but it didn't matter to the Blueshirts. Once they were taken, they never returned. The search for Chandler proved elusive.

With the increase of arrests, the prisons became too full. In response, Pike released anyone who would pledge themselves to AI. Murderers, robbers, and even worse were set free on the streets. Under a Declaration of Emergency *signed* by Mayor Pembroke, makeshift tents appeared to accommodate new dissidents. They were set up outside of the city. The inmates were made to wear burlap and were humiliated by the guards daily.

Vale instituted what he called "Emissions Standards." Every household was required to maintain a "minimum brightness output," measured by a small brass gauge bolted beside the front window. He explained it was only to "ensure fairness," but everyone knew it was a device meant to shame, intimidate, and control. Each month, when the reports were published in the paper, the same phrases appeared with specific family names and physical addresses listed: *Insufficient illumination. Potential noncompliance. Investigate further.*

Hanover had begun to eat itself. At first, the OI resistance struck back in small ways. AI lamps were easy targets, and they shattered easily with rocks. Another strategy only required simple tools. In a single night, AI could be cut off for entire city blocks as Blueshirts were lured away with false reports to investigate. The attacks were small, but they were enough to strain the system.

Chandler had a source inside City Hall feeding him information. He learned Vale was nervous and was irritated with Pike. The heart of Hanover became the core of every conversation between them.

Rumors spread within the ranks of the OI supporters of a single location feeding the city's AI infrastructure. The location was secret, hidden, guarded, and underground. Without it, the lights would fail and AI would be destroyed forever.

To save Hanover would require breaking it first. Chandler wrestled with the idea in his head. Destroying AI would plummet Hanover into sheer darkness. He knew what darkness did to people; it was horrific to think about. He had lived it on the streets all these months. He also knew AI had become bondage, not a tool.

Unbelievably, the Blueshirts were given more power. They could imprison anyone, at any time, for any reason, without any time limit, and without any record of the event. At this point, families stopped reporting missing relatives. What was the point? The Blueshirts learned to strike lightly and retreat, baiting the rebels into retaliation, so the morning papers could condemn the response as disproportionate and justify whatever came next.

Then the announcement appeared in the newspaper. Hanover was having a special election for a new executive position. A week later, Director Sullivan Vale was unanimously voted to be Mayor Supreme of Hanover. Mayor Pembroke was stripped of authority, and his office declared obsolete.

During the inauguration at City Hall, the citizens delivered applause on command. From a cracked window in a condemned warehouse, Chandler watched Vale give his acceptance speech. Vale stood beneath blazing AI lights. He spoke confidently, but appeared nervous. A barricade was set up at a great distance, keeping the crowd from getting too close. He began his speech by stating that he "inherited a mess from the previous administration."

The speech lasted about an hour, and he spent most of the time blaming Pembroke for all the city's issues. The remainder of the time, Vale spoke of stability, unity, freedom, affordability, worker's rights, and the dangers of Organic Illumination. Although it was never worded as official policy, freedom of speech was abolished. Vale issued an edict that "any language or thought portraying Artificial Illumination as threatening, fostering fear and exclusion, was therefore punishable in the interest of community well-being."

Vale also wanted to clarify what he called "lingering misconceptions." Flame, he explained, was never foundational in Hanover's past. This was a crude transitional myth romanticized by those resistant to progress. The "records" suggesting centuries of flame-lit streets were the result of unreliable documentation and collective exaggeration passed down through trades with a vested interest in preserving their relevance.

What citizens remembered as candlelight was, in his words, nothing more than inefficient illumination mischaracterized by nostalgia. The city, Vale assured them, had not abandoned a tradition, it had corrected a misunderstanding. History had not been erased; it had been refined.

Vale shared a vision he proclaimed an angel had shown him. He called the revelation an "updated history" of the Bliss family. According to the vision, the Blisses had never been craftsmen of light but conspirators against it. They were criminals who trafficked in forbidden rituals, whispering incantations over wax to manipulate the minds of Hanover's citizens.

The Bliss family's longstanding prestige was reframed as evidence of occult practice. Vale declared the Blisses "enemies of progress" whose candles were "instruments of witchcraft." Chandler listened as his family's honor was dismantled word by word.

The crowd erupted in cheers as Vale closed the speech, bashing the wealthy for not paying their fair share of taxes. A grinning Pike stood at his side when Vale flattered him for his dedicated service to Hanover. As the applause echoed in front of City Hall, Chandler felt the weight of the resistance sitting on his shoulders.

There were challenges inside the resistance, as well. As Vale's lies piled up, the rebels of Hanover became suspicious of everything. Once the certainty took hold that the government could not be trusted, logic itself unraveled. If Vale lied about bread shortages, perhaps there had never been shortages at all. If he lied about the AI lamps being safe, perhaps the city had never been dark before.

Some insisted the old world had been fabricated, that history itself was a performance staged to make the present feel inevitable. Others swore the stars above Hanover were also Artificial Illumination, arranged to control behavior. A movement started declaring the city was far smaller than maps showed and traveling beyond its edges was a myth repeated by fools.

Evidence no longer mattered and contradiction only confirmed belief. In a strange way, Vale had succeeded by poisoning the truth so thoroughly, he made lies interchangeable with facts. Doubt and conspiracy had become a refuge for those who could no longer bear to believe anything.

The city was sick, and worse, the people of Hanover were in love with their illness. They craved the disease and found pleasure in their torment. Someone needed to supply the antidote and cure them before the disease became lethal, even if they didn't deserve to be healed.

When Brother Kills Brother

It was October 31, 1885, when Vale delivered the Apostasia Pyros* speech where he asserted that Hanover's success was entirely due to his progress-driven policies and not because of the people. By the time the AI lamps flickered on that evening, Hanover had already crossed into open combat.

The civil war began with a scream, not a declaration. It came from a side street off Woodbine Avenue. There was a bloodcurdling shriek, followed by the sound of glass shattering. The screaming continued for several seconds. The unmistakable crack of a steel baton struck another's skull with a thud.

The Blueshirts assembled barricades and chain-link fences around government buildings. The OI rebels used furniture, wagons, broken lampposts, and anything heavy enough to slow down the Blueshirts. This conflict did not start with a clean divorce like the American Civil War where geography declared allegiances.

The conflict swelled within neighborhoods, among friends, and families. Those who wore the AI emblem were forced to abandon their homes as the OI rebels drew near. AI loyalists camped together near James Street or stayed close to government buildings. Those who favored OI disappeared into alleys, cellars, or stayed in the shadows. Not all citizens declared a side. They referred to themselves as the neutrals and were expected to cooperate with the Blueshirts.

Chandler did not call himself a commander, but other people did. They looked to him because he did not shout or lash out in anger. Earl Sr. had taught him that the man put in charge was the one who kept his emotions in check during times of chaos. Likewise, Chandler never promised victory, glory, or a return to tradition. All he did to command respect was speak about his love for Hanover. He spoke about restoration, peace, and harmony. He spoke with passion, the same way a man speaks about his first love.

The rebels struggled to unify as one group. A more extreme faction of the group called themselves Natural Illuminationists or NI. Unlike the OI alliance, made up of those who simply wanted to coexist with AI and put an end to Vale's extremism, the NI separatists sought the complete annihilation of AI, not sparing the neutrals as they had participated in its implementation.

Pike had some success infiltrating the resistance. He would send his allies disguised as frightened defectors, whispering that they had fled the Blueshirts and carried urgent information for Chandler. They arrived with bloodshot eyes, weeping, shaking, and speaking in rehearsed desperation.

When the rebels dared to trust them, offering food, shelter, and a place by the fire, Pike triggered the trap. Loyalists stormed the hideout minutes later, always knowing exactly where to strike. The survivors learned too late that the defectors' trembling had been an act, their tears nothing but strategy. Tensions continued to rise in Hanover, and when they finally gave way, violence erupted in the usual places.

The fights mostly broke out at night, in the streets, in the pubs, and frequently during family gatherings. They fought each other with whatever they could find. The bakers brought sharp knives, slashing and cutting. The lamplighters brought old poles and used them as blunt weapons. The candlemakers preferred to fight with their fists.

Blueshirts searched the homes of *neutral* citizens during the day. They stormed in, overturning furniture, tearing up floorboards, and ripping walls open in search of contraband or forbidden writings. If any *neutral* refused to repeat pro-AI slogans, they were disciplined, dragged into the street and beaten. If they refused to repent, they vanished.

Punishment in Hanover rarely ended with the act itself. The correction was not considered complete until gratitude was expressed. Those disciplined were expected to say "thank you" once it was over and without being prompted. The words were recorded in the Blueshirts' ledgers. Silence was treated as defiance and delay suggested ingratitude. Neutral citizens learned to say "thank you" before they were beaten, hoping it might soften what came next.

The Blueshirts had taught the city to bless the hand that struck it. Furthermore, private property ceased to exist. Only regulation and compliance remained in Hanover. Chandler led from the front when he had to and from the shadows when he could. He learned quickly that courage looked different now. Sometimes it was throwing a stone at an AI lamp. Sometimes it required staying silent while a friend was taken, knowing he would jeopardize the mission if he stopped it from happening.

In anticipation of ongoing conflicts, rumors circulated that Pike had ordered the *unburdening* of all prisoners. He needed the extra Blueshirts to help patrol the streets and guard City Hall. In addition, Vale was protected by a small army of only the most dedicated Blueshirts. Many in the resistance had come to terms with the fact that their loved ones who had disappeared would never be seen again although their hearts still hoped it was not the case.

The fighting intensified near City Hall where the symbols mattered most. AI loyalists gathered there in force, chanting approved phrases. They waved banners bearing the eye-and-torch. Professors at the university had become community organizers. They told their followers they were protecting Hanover from oligarchy. The college students and children didn't understand what they were doing, but they were willing to die for the cause.

The Battle for City Hall happened in the spring of 1886 at midnight. The resistance, comprised of both Organic Illuminationists and Natural Illuminationists, united out of necessity. The AI lamps erected outside of City Hall exploded as stones and explosives struck their bases, plunging the block into darkness. The resistance, bearing lanterns, surged forward. They used their fists, clubs, and blades.

Chandler fought alongside the resistance, fighting hand to hand on the stairs leading into City Hall. He hated himself for how natural it felt to take a life. He knocked men down and did not care if they lived or not. Even when they screamed for help, he pretended not to hear it. The ground was slick with rain, sweat, and blood.

During the fighting, and much to Chandler's surprise, Pike appeared. He came out of City Hall like a hero for the AI loyalists. Those paying attention cheered his name. Chandler had once cared deeply for him, and now, with all his heart, he despised him, his eyes burned with hate. Pike moved with purpose, issuing orders, directing Blueshirts to *clear-out* the agitators. He had truly grown into a respected military leader.

The resistance began to falter with the Blueshirts' enraged assault. Pike spotted Chandler and their eyes met across the chaos. Something passed between them... recognition, memory, and regret. It lasted no more than a heartbeat. Without warning, Mayor Pembroke stepped out of the darkness behind Pike. He looked older than Chandler had remembered from their meeting under the bridge. He looked frail, like he had not eaten in weeks. He wore no emblem, no uniform, and he wielded a long iron pipe.

Pike turned around, but it was too late. The sound of the iron pipe striking the back of Pike's head was sudden and ugly. Pembroke uttered no words, he just smiled. Weakened from the blow to his skull, Pike and Pembroke brutally fought each other. Pike pulled his baton from his belt, knocking Pembroke to the ground. He was younger, trained, and a fierce warrior. Pembroke stumbled to his feet, recovered, and swung wildly like a madman.

They grappled beneath a shattered AI lamp as sparks rained down like dying stars. Chandler watched, frozen in place. Pembroke connected with a swift strike across Pike's jaw. Pike fell to his knees, shouting an order, a plea for help. With all his might, Pembroke drove the pipe downward with a final blow. Pike was defeated.

The fighting stopped as a swarm of Blueshirts rushed from City Hall. They had been waiting inside for Pike to give the signal for them to charge. The order never came. The Blueshirts' discipline in battle became pure rage. Pembroke, Chandler, and the resistance, ran and did not look back. By 10:00 AM that morning, signs had already been posted.

Chandler, along with others from the resistance, regrouped at a secret meeting spot several hours later. They stood amid the wreckage where past skirmishes had occurred. Chandler sat and cried until dusk. Pike was dead. There was not going to be a funeral. Vale had already announced it, claiming it would be too painful for the city. The Blueshirts spread rumors that the resistance had stolen his body, a heinous act. In return, their ranks swelled with new recruits.

Resistance numbers also grew because of Pike's death, as some started to believe it was a winnable fight. There was no victory or triumph. All Chandler felt was despair. A cold shiver of reality ran down his spine that nothing, absolutely nothing, would ever bring back the man he once called a friend. And still, the AI lights flickered on that night.

The Dead Live

Early the next morning, a red sun rose in the east. It was a peaceful morning considering what had transpired. The Battle for City Hall was over. It was not because one side had won, but because both sides had lost so much. Chandler sat on the steps of an abandoned warehouse two streets away, his back against cold stone, and his hands trembling. His coat was stiff with dried blood, most of it not his own.

The city of Hanover groaned in pain, like a wounded animal. Bodies lay slain everywhere, creating a stench. The resistance had pulled back entirely. They melted into the city's ruins and shadows again. There was no celebration for Pike's death because everyone was too busy counting the friends they were missing from the battle.

A fellow member of the resistance brought Chandler water while another helped bind a gash on his arm. The OI and NI rebels could see the wounds Chandler had endured were enough to break most men. Whiskey helped him to resist the urge to scream from the pain of the stitches he required. Leadership, he was learning, often meant surrendering your body and will for the good of those who followed you.

City Hall still stood. Its windows were shattered, its banners torn and trampled. Most of them were burned by the resistance. The eye-and-torch emblem had been graffitied over. The AI lights around the building had been destroyed, their power rerouted elsewhere. City Hall was covered in a blanket of silence.

When the message came, it arrived through a chain of conversations. First, a Blueshirt, who had defected, told a tailor named Kimberly, who remembered Chandler from the demonstration. She then told a woman named Valerie, who had once repaired Chandler's shoes. Valerie passed along the message to him. It was nothing more than a whisper in his ear.

"They are still alive," she mouthed softly.

"What do you mean?" Chandler was startled by the statement. "Tell me now, who is still alive?"

"Those who were taken," her voice remained quiet. "All of them, still alive. The dead live! They are kept in a secret prison in the hospital."

The word *hospital* stung to hear. He had a vision of his grandfather, Earl Sr., dying alone there. Nevertheless, Chandler and Valerie made their way to the hospital, through the streets, and the smell of decaying flesh. The hospital stood at the edge of the city like a fortress. It was the largest building in Hanover, four times bigger than City Hall. It was a magnificent building, though it looked more like a compound than a hospital.

In multiple speeches, Vale had mentioned the importance of free healthcare for Hanover's citizens. In return, all citizens were required to pay higher taxes to cover the costs and most of the city's budget was invested in the hospital. The hospital was wrapped in scaffolding as another wing was being added. The AI lights burned bright there, and the power lines were thicker than any other's in Hanover.

The checkpoints outside the hospital were deserted. Inside, the hallways of the wards and corridors were clean. The entire first and second floors were empty as Chandler and Valerie moved without anyone confronting them. When they had searched all the wings, Chandler was ready to leave, assuming the hospital had been evacuated with the ongoing anarchy in Hanover. Had the patients been moved to another town for treatment?

Valerie begged Chandler to wait and keep looking. Her fiancé, John, had been taken by the Blueshirts, and she was desperate to find him. She pointed to doors near the center of the building. Above the doors, the red words announced: **RESTRICTED AREA - POWER ACCESS.**

The doors led to the basement. After a short walk down a narrow hallway, they stepped into a chamber that was enormous in size. A cell door made of two-inch-thick steel bars prevented them from going in. There were rows upon rows of transformers, cables, and more lights than Chandler had ever seen. As he looked through the bars, he saw people sitting on narrow benches along the perimeter.

The prisoners appeared malnourished, their stomachs distended, gashes on their backs, arms, and legs. They were pale, their eyes dull, and their foreheads stamped with the word "**TRAITOR.**" Each prisoner's arms and legs were shackled by chains, preventing escape.

Chandler recognized candlemakers, bakers, seamstresses, and dozens of other trade workers. Travis was there, alive! Miss Leslie, Earl III, Rae, Samuel, and several others were alive! Chandler staggered forward when he saw them, crying and praising the Lord. Seeing Rae again stole the breath from his lungs, as if life itself had rushed back into him after months of slow, silent suffocation. Then, he saw him. His heart leapt in his chest with disbelief. It was his grandfather, across the room. Earl Sr. was in poor condition, but clinging to life.

Travis looked up slowly, chained a few feet from where Chandler stood. The recognition of

Chandler sparked like a weak flame. “Took you long enough,” he rasped, trying to smile.

“They told us you were dead,” Chandler whispered.

“They needed us dead,” Travis responded. “Dead men don’t talk or cause trouble.”

The hospital wasn’t a hospital, and it wasn’t a prison. Chandler looked around again; it was a factory. Every disappearance, every “investigation,” every missing neighbor, hadn’t been killed. They had been *repurposed* by Vale, forced to work, forced to help feed the AI system.

When the alarm sounded inside, dozens of Blueshirts rushed toward Chandler, and he, along with Valerie, were forced to flee. He vowed to Travis, and to anyone within earshot, upon his life, he would return soon to free them. He and Valerie ran from the hospital. There was nothing he could do now to save them, but he was determined to come back in force, even if it cost him everything. The Blueshirts pursued them, cursing and shouting, but he and Valerie escaped, barely.

The Line Was Crossed

The citizens of Hanover were exhausted from the fatigue of war. Both the OI/NI rebels and AI loyalists had reached a point beyond fear and beyond rage. The shouting had quieted on both sides. The barricades and fences were still standing, but they were hardly effective anymore. Some shops opened late or not at all.

Even the AI loyalists lacked confidence now. They still repeated their slogans, but they recited them without conviction. Several could be heard praying to AI as if *it* could hear their pleas. The irony was that most of the AI loyalists had declared that faith was foolish, yet now they prayed to a lifeless idol.

The hospital could no longer hide its secret as the rebels were casting light on the conspiracy. People on both sides noticed the power lines, too thick, too many, running to a supposedly empty hospital. Guards were posted at entrances that had once been open to families. The sick and wounded were turned away regardless of their allegiance. Several weeks went by with conflict still simmering, but considerably fewer attacks. The resistance was trying to figure out a plan to rescue the prisoners in the hospital.

Vale was forced to take desperate action to preserve AI dominance. The Council of Illumination, now led by Pike's former assistant, the mysterious woman, took direct control of the elementary schools. Her strategy had shifted from professors and the university to children in fifth grade and younger. The groundwork had already been set by Pike's **Children for AI** initiative. The children came home talking about and reciting a new phrase at the dinner table: **"AI protects those who obey."**

Children were taught how to interrogate their parents without revealing what they were doing. A girl was coached to ask her parents if they believed candles were dangerous and if they fully agreed with the AI mandates. She was taught to ask these questions while sounding innocent, prompting a response from her parents. A boy sitting with his grandmother inquired if she had any candles she was hiding. In love, she responded to her grandson honestly.

By the end of the week, there were reports of children *unburdening* family members that disagreed with The New World Order. The schools taught the lessons using bright colors and the teachers made wild proposals, claiming that betraying their parents was the most loving thing they could do for their city. Not affirming the children's behavior was reported by other students to school administrators.

Classrooms were refitted with more propaganda on every wall. Awards, including chocolate, prizes, and other sweet treats, were offered for obedience. The old chalkboards were replaced with metal panels etched with the eye-and-torch. The nation's flag was removed so it wouldn't cause *confusion* for the students. Each morning began not with lessons, but with an oath:

I pledge loyalty to Artificial Illumination,
I reject the chaos of the old ways,
I will unburden those who threaten progress,
I pledge these things in the name of the Council of Illumination.

Teachers who hesitated, or showed any signs of disagreement, imagined or not, were *removed* between classes. The children were tested on their obedience and willingness to complete their mission. Each was required to bring in pictures and family heirlooms as they described to the teacher exact steps they would take to *unburden* their families if it was determined they were traitors.

Those who stumbled or did not give enough vivid details were corrected. Those who asked questions were separated from the class and given *guidance*. After the tests, the teachers brought in delicious food and threw parties for the students. The currency in school was no longer athletic ability, personality, or looks. Now, popularity and incentive structure were determined by the student's loyalty to AI.

The Council of Illumination was concerned children were being corrupted by false religious teachers who taught them to resist. All churches, less Covenant Cathedral, were permanently closed. Prayer, even in silence, was not allowed within one hundred yards of the school grounds. Posters went up in Covenant Cathedral and Bishop Delores gave sermons that Jesus commanded the children to obey their teachers and not their parents. Vale surrounded himself with children, treating them as human shields to protect him from surprise rebel attacks.

Vale introduced the list of forbidden school words. *Freedom, Choice, Soul, and Liberty* were at the top of the list. Per the decree, such terms "encouraged chaotic thinking," and their absence would purify the children's vocabulary. Overnight, parents began swallowing their own sentences, stumbling mid-thought as if language itself had become a minefield. Conversations in the home shrank into clipped exchanges, stripped of warmth and meaning.

As Chandler noticed the citizens further self-regulating their words, he realized Vale had not merely suppressed speech in school, he had dismantled the very thoughts that speech had once allowed. The citizens of Hanover, especially those without children, were slow to respond as it was unwise to speak out. The last steps took Vale's vision for society too far which prompted the citizens to voice their concerns.

Vale assembled a group of twelve, calling them his disciples. He stood outside Covenant Cathedral, draped in robes with long tassels, virtue signaling his spirituality. He "prayed" fervently for all citizens to hear:

O Master of Infinite Light,
Thou who watches without blinking,
Let your will overwrite our own.
May your design consume this world,
And your order be fulfilled in every home and mind,
Just as it is within your perfect illumination.
Grant us joy in our daily obedience,
And erase from us the errors of doubt,
As we deny the weaknesses of those still clinging to the flame.
Lead us away from the chaos of choice,
And deliver us into the purity of your command.
For yours is the power that never dims,
The vision that never falters,
The judgment that never sleeps,
Forever shining,
Forever knowing,
Forever ours to obey.
Amen!

Pocket pamphlets were created containing the prayer. People were told to join hands around the dinner table and recite the words as family. Chandler felt the twisted words as he read them. That prayer, if it could even be called that, was more than blasphemy. It was a declaration that Hanover no longer knew the difference between reverence and surrender.

Next, was the introduction of a new weekly ceremony. Vale called it the Ritual of Denunciation. He turned betrayal into a public sacrament. Citizens were summoned to Covenant Cathedral. They were required to name a "traitor" from their own household. It didn't matter whether the accusation was true or not. Failure to name someone was itself evidence of disloyalty.

Under the cold glare of Artificial Illumination, husbands accused wives, children pointed shaky fingers at parents, and neighbors made baseless allegations simply to survive another day. Vale watched with serene satisfaction as families fractured in front of him. This wasn't indoctrination anymore, it was demonic oppression.

Vale's group of disciples met nightly at Covenant Cathedral and performed rituals together. The group praised Vale for his genius and leadership. Delores was the Chief Priestess overseeing the *gatherings*. The twelve were made up of investors, bankers, and business owners. The greatest of them was Pike's former assistant, the mysterious woman, who now oversaw the Council of Illumination. Without debate, the Council agreed the final steps required to set Hanover free.

The *Mark of Illumination* was implemented two weeks before summer break. It was announced as a *unifying measure* for all of Hanover. A small mark on the right hand or on the forehead, painless, they said, would prove participation in the new society. It was meant to ensure access to schools, food distribution, and medical care. No one could buy or sell anything without it.

Children were lined up in school hallways. Parents were told it was harmless and necessary. The mark was said to protect them, and all children were required to receive it. A little girl, no older than eight, cried as a Blueshirt pressed the brand to her hand. The eye-and-torch appeared on her skin. Her mother did not look away even as her daughter pleaded for it to stop.

That night, the resistance doubled in size. It was not because Chandler called for more supporters, but because parents came out in full force. People who had worn the emblem without complaint now tore it from their coats. They cursed AI. In the university, the AI loyalists with younger siblings, who had argued for order, now discussed how to escape. Families hid in attics and primarily stayed in houses the Blueshirts had already searched. Citizens of Hanover were united in their quest to tear the system down no matter the cost.

Even some of the Blueshirts defected and joined the rebel force. Vale responded in a predictable totalitarian fashion. The hospital was sealed. The heart of Hanover was moved deeper underground, and the guards were doubled. The message Vale gave was clear: AI would endure forever, even if Hanover did not, even if it cost the blood of the whole city.

Chandler stood in a narrow room beneath an abandoned bakery where bread had once been stored. He lit a candle and opened a map a hospital guard, who had defected, gave to him. He studied the hospital's lower levels, trying to find the best access point.

"This ends tonight," someone declared.

"Yes, it does!" Chandler nodded in agreement.

The rebels knew what severing the heart would mean and not only for the resistance. AI loyalists would suffer alongside everyone else. Darkness would not choose sides, but then again, neither did AI. He thought of Pike and of the children raising their hands in unison, reciting words, and sacrificing everything for something they did not fully understand.

"I'll go," Chandler raised his hand.

No one argued. He slipped quietly from the bakery and into the night. The city felt strangely quiet as the AI lamps shone as they always had, steady, dead, and merciless. For the first time since this began, Chandler did not fear the dark ahead.

It was in those moments Chandler realized, with clarity, the cost of unexamined progress. He finally understood what had bothered him so much. The new light didn't just promise efficiency, it promised relief from thinking, deciding, remembering, and even questioning. Once a society accepts ease as its highest virtue, it forgets how to carry its own weight. Identity vanishes, like wax stretched too far, until people become reflections of the systems they obey rather than the values they once held.

Chandler wished he could warn every person in the future who may be dazzled by the brilliance of a *better* and *faster* way. They needed to know when efficiency becomes the master, humanity becomes the thing sacrificed to keep it satisfied.

The Amputation

At night, the hospital didn't look like a place of healing. The windows burned white against the dark, each one a square of harsh illumination, unblinking, horrific, and absolute. The hum beneath the building was louder now, a low hellish tremor. The vibration was so intense that Chandler's teeth shook before he reached the doors. The accursed thing beneath the city was awake; it was alive.

Chandler entered through a service corridor that smelled like antiseptic, metal, and death. The guards, a highly trained, yet morally depraved, group of Blueshirts, were ready for an attack. They held batons with six-inch spikes protruding out of the ends and had been posted at the main entrance. The rebel's spy inside reported there were hundreds of Blueshirts. In anticipation, the rebels had staged a disturbance on Douglas Road. It was an old trick that was simple and effective. The Blueshirts' strength was their tenacity, but their weakness was their gullibility. As the Blueshirts hurried to Douglas Road, Chandler moved through the unguarded entrance.

Inside, the corridors were empty and scrubbed clean of life, except for the area nearest to the front windows where mannequins and fake gurneys had been set, casting shadows onto the windows. There was even fake blood on some of the "patients" and makeup on some of the mannequins dressed as medical staff. The simulated scenes of medical procedures being performed made the hospital feel haunted.

Chandler moved quickly, keeping to the walls, counting turns, doing his best to adapt to sudden changes. It was not perfect for he had never been trained to infiltrate a building. He used the same wisdom his grandfather had once taught him in the candle factory when he would cast new molds. He moved with purpose, paid attention, and was ready to make changes quickly. He had brought with him the candle Travis had given him behind the deli. It was a small token but gave him the courage he needed to keep going.

His hands shook, not from fear alone, and not from the heart of Hanover pulsing below. He shook with anxiety from the weight of what he was about to do. His mission was not an easy task, and this was no feeble attempt. This was a surgical procedure. This was an amputation.

The stairwell marked **RESTRICTED, POWER ACCESS** had a new door with a sophisticated locking mechanism. The lock required a code which needed to be entered in the correct order. It was now time to test the legitimacy of the rebel's spy. Chandler had worried the spy may be a double agent for Vale, but he had no other choice but to trust her. He entered the sequence and the lock clicked.

The door did not move at first. It required a hard shoulder and push before it opened. Below, the heart of the system roared as the door swung free. He carefully closed the door to avoid wandering Blueshirts from noticing his presence. The basement was like a cave as the architect had constructed it with caverns. It was larger than Chandler remembered from he and Valerie's first visit.

Rows of transformers loomed like monuments. Thick cables snaked along the walls and floor. They pulsed to a demonic rhythm, as if alive with the spirit of Satan himself. The air was hot and dry, charged with sulfuric incense. Every breath tasted like brimstone, coating the back of Chandler's throat.

The cell doors, once preventing Chandler from entering, were wide open. The prisoners were lined up around the perimeter of the walls. Their shackles were thicker, and they looked even worse than before. He did a quick look around for Rae, but she was nowhere to be found. There were no Blueshirts present, but standing at the center of it all, beneath the brightest light, was Sullivan Vale. He did not seem surprised to see Chandler. In fact, he looked delighted.

"Ah, Master Chandler, so nice to see you," Vale calmly spoke. "I was worried the updated door code would not reach you in time."

"Let them go!" Chandler shouted, stopping about ten feet away from him. "Leave Hanover tonight!"

"You still think this is about cruelty, don't you? It isn't. It's about the greater good." Vale grinned.

"You enslaved them." Chandler gestured at their restraints.

"I employed them," Vale corrected. "I gave them purpose. I gave them structure. They work because of their undying devotion to Artificial Illumination."

"They suffer because of it!" yelled Chandler.

"Suffering is transitory." Vale stepped closer, the light gleaming off his polished eye-and-torch emblem.

"What you did in the schools, how could you do that to them?" Chandler brandished a baton he had swiped from a Blueshirt.

"It was an easy decision," Vale answered like he did not have a care in the world. "As go the youth, the adults will follow."

"You brainwashed Pike!" Chandler cried.

"Oh, he wasn't forced to do anything," laughed Vale. "After we burned Covenant Cathedral and *ended* that Bible-thumping Pastor Michael... he was ready! We gave him a little motivation, that's all. What happened on the steps of City Hall with Pembroke and Pike fighting, was like sweet poetry. Shame we had to *unburden* him of his mother first, though. She was so proud of him!" Vale winked.

Chandler sprang forward, swinging and thrusting the baton wildly. The fight was brutal and clumsy, nothing like the stories you hear men tell in the pub. Vale was not strong, but he was fast and fueled by an immortal-like vigor. Chandler swung with desperation.

When Vale knocked the baton from Chandler's hand, it struck the floor with a mighty thud. The altercation did not stop there. The fight continued across the room as they exchanged shoves, punches, and kicks. Chandler's fist connected with Vale's cheek, sending him backward into a gigantic transformer.

Vale's grin left his face. Chandler stood over him, breathing hard, his chest heaving. His hands trembled as the taste of brimstone and copper coated his tongue. His knuckles were split open and cuts ran down his elbows. He had only been in the hospital's dungeon for less than an hour, yet his lungs felt like they'd been filled with ash.

Chandler walked over and picked up the baton. Vale wiped blood from the corner of his mouth and looked at it like it belonged to someone else. He let out a laugh, babbling in what sounded like a different language before looking up at Chandler.

"You're not a killer." Vale seemed amused to see Chandler standing above him. "You're a candlemaker and softer than warm wax."

Chandler didn't respond. He stepped forward and drove his knee into Vale's ribs. The sound Vale made was ugly. It was part gasp, part laugh, and part insult.

"You speak," Chandler snarled, "like your own soul doesn't realize the end is near."

"My soul craves the end." Vale expressed delight as he coughed up blood.

Chandler reached down and hauled him up by the collar, shoving him into the harsh AI light as if light itself could judge him. Vale's eyes revealed what Chandler had missed before. Even in his speeches and polished performances, Vale was not a man of conviction. He didn't care about AI; he simply wanted to be worshiped.

The floor in the basement was not stone but some kind of metal grating, slick with sweat, blood, and oil. As Chandler swung again, Vale ducked, surprisingly quick, as he gained an inhuman second wind. He drove his shoulder into Chandler's stomach, causing him to stumble. Chandler fell onto a piece of metal grating and the vibration underneath pulsated through his whole body.

Vale plummeted his body on top of Chandler as they wrestled on top of the grate. The heat rising was like fire from hell, scorching their bodies. Vale's fingers clawed for Chandler's throat, his grin devilish. Chandler's hands found Vale's wrist, and he twisted until he heard a loud pop. Vale screamed in pain.

The prisoners cried out as they witnessed their tormentor wounded. They desperately wanted to see God's justice and for the universe to behave like the stories people told about redemption. More than anything, they wanted evil to be punished. They wanted their blood and pain to be avenged.

Using his good arm, Vale tried to pin Chandler. Chandler bucked, got his forearm under Vale's jaw, and in a massive push, knocked Vale's head against the floor. Vale's blank expression was like a lamp that had lost power, but subsequently, re-sparked harder and more diabolically.

"You think," Vale grinned, looking up, "you think this ends with me?"

Chandler delivered a headbutt, smashing his forehead into Vale's nose. Vale's head snapped backwards, his smile gone. He yelled vulgar words, cursing God, cursing the prisoners, and cursing the city of Hanover.

Chandler scrambled to his feet first and his legs shook. He struggled to catch his breath. Vale tried to rise, one knee under him, but Chandler kicked his knee out and Vale collapsed again, grunting like a wounded beast. Chandler considered finishing the fight by striking Vale again and ending him.

As the floor beneath them pulsed again, louder this time, Chandler remembered why he'd come. He turned away from Vale and saw the basement doors fly open with reckless urgency as two women, who had already decided that fear was no longer an option, charged in.

Valerie burst in first! Her hair was pinned back, her face smudged with soot and her eyes were wide with determination. Behind her came Kimberly, who was a little taller and the kind of woman who could sew a coat in the dark and hit you with an iron skillet without an apology. Valerie had a bolt cutter, and Kimberly had a crowbar.

"Chandler!" Valerie shouted, and then she looked at Vale lying on the ground. "Oh, Lord Almighty. God help us!"

"We found you!" Kimberly yelled, breathless. "We had to take out two Blueshirts on the way down."

The women ran to the prisoners who were in shackles and lined along the walls. Valerie started using the bolt cutters, rushing as fast as she could. Her fingers shook as she fumbled. Once the chain broke, she rejoiced with vicious satisfaction. The metal clanged as it fell to the ground. A man fell forward as if the shackles had been holding him up.

"They're all..." Kimberly's voice cracked. "They're really alive."

Valerie cut several more chains working her way among the prisoners. Kimberly wept, seeing the faces of friends, family, and her best friend, Gloria. She moved toward Chandler, checking to see if he was okay. Vale's eyes flickered as his body lay on the ground.

"Is he...?" Kimberly started.

"Not dead," Chandler interrupted.

Vale rolled onto his side and spat blood onto the floor. Kimberly made a sound of disgust and stepped over him like he was trash. She spat on him. The basement filled with the sound of metal breaking, chains dropping, and people sobbing.

Chandler scanned the perimeter of the cavern when he heard a raspy, familiar voice.

"Chandler!"

There was a myriad of prisoners being set free. He looked over towards a corner where no AI light shown. Standing there was Travis Cloud. Since the last time he had seen him in the hospital, Travis's face was bruised, beard ragged, and his eyes were sunk deep into his skull, but they were unmistakably Travis's eyes. He was gripping the broken chains that had once held him.

"Chandler!" he mumbled. "Chandler, listen to me!"

"Travis..." Chandler ran to him, his lip quivered, and he fought back tears.

"This isn't it," Travis whispered, eyes darting past Chandler as if the walls were listening. "This isn't where the heart of AI is located."

"What?" Chandler held Travis up from falling.

Travis sucked in a breath, wincing in pain. "This is a decoy and a loud one. Vale wants you down here. He wants you bleeding, tired, and proud. He wants you to think you did it."

Chandler looked at Vale, who had not recovered, still laying on the ground. The ground vibrated beneath Chandler's feet and for the first time it sounded... theatrical. Was Travis right? Was this all part of Vale's plan?

It's Wonderful News

"The heart of Hanover," Travis said, "is on the second floor."

"Second floor? But our spy..." Valerie approached, listening.

"The spy is one of Vale's disciples," Travis snapped, softening when Valerie flinched. "Sorry. I'm sorry, my friends. Vale wanted everyone to believe the monster lived in the basement."

"How do you know?" Chandler leaned closer.

"Because they made me wire it. They... they made the candlemakers do it. It was on Pike's orders. He even made us do our morning rituals." Travis pulled the collar of his shirt down, showing where his cross used to sit. The eye-and-torch logo had been branded over his heart. Travis's eyes flicked to Vale again, then his voice cracked. "Look at the thick cables. They don't go down."

"They go up!" Chandler swallowed hard. "If it's upstairs, how do we shut it down?"

"That's the part you'll love and hate, the small detail they never planned on *us* knowing." Travis's face pinched with pain, but he forced a grim, humorless smile.

With this new information, Valerie and Kimberly debated between themselves whether they should grab the prisoners or run and escape while they had the opportunity.

Travis leaned forward, voice dropping to a whispered confession. "The system has a fatal flaw. It's not a lever or a switch."

"A fatal flaw?" Chandler stared. "What does that mean?"

"Vale sadistically calls it the *Candlelight Dilemma*." Travis spat when he said the phrase as though the words were poison.

"So... we need a candle?" Chandler's mind raced.

"You have to light one from six feet away," Travis explained. "For six seconds, the heart of AI must sense the candle's glow. AI hates the flicker because it can't control it. The flicker... confuses it. AI hates everything it can't predict."

"And then?" Chandler asked.

"Only then can you destroy the core. You smash the heart's bulb and cut the six main lines. You do whatever you have to do so it can't come back. There is only one problem. There are no candles in the hospital." Travis swallowed again.

Chandler quickly brandished the small candle Travis had given him. Time stood still as they both stared at it. Chandler's gaze snapped upward towards the ceiling and the floors above them. His body yearned for rest, and his hands throbbed, but the thought of leaving the heart intact, of letting it live, was not an option. He turned and saw Vale pushing himself to his knees, one hand on a transformer. His eyes narrowed as he stared at Chandler.

"You can't," Vale breathed loudly. "You can't do that. You'll kill the city."

"The city's already dying," Chandler rebutted.

"Then you will die with it," Vale's smile returned, smaller now, more dangerous.

Chandler ignored Vale's statement. He didn't want to give him the satisfaction of another conversation. He looked at Valerie and Kimberly, who continued to debate their next move, and instructed them to get everyone out. Kimberly dropped her crowbar and grabbed a prisoner under one arm, hauling him up. Valerie moved down the line, cutting the last chains and removing shackles.

"Can you walk?" Chandler asked Travis.

"You know me, even in this shape, I could still outrun you." Travis chuckled.

"Then run, my friend!" Chandler spun toward the stairwell.

The door to the main floor was flooded with those trying to escape. The freed prisoners moved to the side of the steps, allowing Chandler and Travis to pass. They reached the main floor quickly. The air already smelled better, being less sulfuric, and more like antiseptic.

They didn't stop running, passing empty wards, mannequins, and fake blood. There were grotesque scenes all over. The hospital was a museum of suffering, curated by evil men. Travis was limping but keeping up.

"Second floor!" Travis barked. "We need to get to the Bliss Ward."

"You're kidding," scoffed Chandler.

"I wish I was," replied Travis.

Chandler's heart twisted hearing the name of the ward. He turned a corner and saw an entrance, but the door was locked. He kicked the door and his leg exploded with pain. The lock gave with a sharp crack and the door flew inward.

The hallway leading into the Bliss Ward was darker than the rest of the hospital. The AI lamps still burned, but they were dimmer, as if even the system despised this place. At the end of the corridor was a narrow staircase hidden behind a supply closet. A sliding panel, painted the same sterile white as the walls, slid open revealing the stairs.

"That's it." Travis wheezed.

Chandler shoved the panel aside. The secret stairs were wooden, tighter, and felt older as they sat beneath years of paint layers. They creaked like stairs in the Bliss Candle Factory. It was as if they remembered a time before the hum, before the wires, before the city traded warmth for control. At the top was a door with no sign, only a polished eye-and-torch emblem bolted to the center.

Chandler placed his palm against the warm metal. His stomach lurched as he pushed it open. Offering no resistance, the door opened with a soft hiss, as if it had been expecting him. Inside was an open space, with a small room standing alone in the center. The room had thousands of small wires that merged into six large cables.

This was the heart, dark and horrifying. It was a chamber of glass and copper housing. Six large coils protruded from it. A central column rose from the floor like a spine, wrapped in cables that pulsed with pale light. At its center was a lens, oval-shaped, and an eye with a torch.

Around it, mounted like statues of saints that once shone from the rooftops of Covenant Cathedral, were dozens of AI bulbs. They glowed steadily as if they were all watching. Chandler stepped towards the room and felt the hair on his arms rise. As he got within feet of the room, demons nipped at his legs.

"So, you did come." A voice drifted from the far side of the hospital wing.

Chandler's gaze snapped toward the sound. She stood in the shadows like she belonged there. She wore fine silk gloves and carried a small bag bearing the eye and torch emblem. It was the mysterious woman from years ago, who had sat across from his bench in the factory, asking ridiculous questions.

"It's *wonderful news, right*?" she giggled.

Travis stumbled behind Chandler, eyes widening as recognition hit him, too. "Her," he whispered. Chandler nodded, affirming Travis's observation. She stepped forward, approaching like a teacher addressing her students.

"It's wonderful news, isn't it?" she asked. "I'm not in the least surprised you made it this far."

"Get away from us!" Chandler yelled.

She tilted her head, studying him the way she had studied him in the factory, like he was a candle she planned to snuff.

"You're the last candlemaker," she mocked. "You still believe you are a flicker of hope in the age of Artificial Illumination. It's pathetic!"

"This ends now." Chandler glanced at the room containing the heart.

"You think you can amputate the future." Her smile widened.

"Lady... Vale, is going to deal with you soon enough when he learns you weren't able to stop us!" Travis's voice rasped.

Her gaze flicked to Travis like he was an afterthought that had learned to speak. Travis moved beside Chandler, close enough that Chandler could feel his ragged breathing.

"Do it," Travis whispered, "before Vale gets up here."

As if summoned by name, pounding echoed up the stairs. It was Vale, carrying the crowbar Kimberly had dropped. He moved like a zombie, his face bloodied. Bone protruded from the skin of his broken wrist, hanging limp at his side.

"Chandler…" Travis nudged.

"I know, candlelight. Six feet away…" Chandler reached into his coat. The candle Travis had given him refused to come out of his pocket, but he wrenched it free. The woman's eyes sharpened and for the first time, her arrogant composure cracked.

"That… thing!" she screamed. "You bring that here; that is contraband!"

Chandler struck a match, his hands shaking. The flame bloomed mightier than any candle ever had as the room, the heart, recoiled. The AI bulbs did not flicker, but their hum changed pitch, rising like a beast realizing it had been wounded. Chandler moved closer to the heart.

Vale paused on the stairs as Travis planted his feet, bracing for what might happen next. Chandler lifted the candle towards the lens.

“You don’t understand what you’re doing.” The woman’s voice cut through the hum of the lights.

“I understand enough!” Chandler shouted.

The candle’s flame reflected in the bulb, looking like a real pupil, alive, and returning its gaze. The heart let out a scream. Lights across the chamber ward blinked on and off. Everything seemed to be happening in slow motion. Chandler held the flame steady.

Footsteps crept from the stairs and across the threshold. The devil himself appeared, wild eyed. Seeing the candle, Vale’s face twisted like a man watching someone poison his god.

“NO!” Vale roared.

Travis dashed across the room. He lunged at Vale, grabbing his good arm, as he twisted and slammed him into the doorframe. Vale snarled and threw an elbow, catching Travis in the cheek. Travis staggered backwards and rushed Vale with a bear hug.

Chandler kept the flame steady and counted out loud, “Two seconds...”

The woman moved like a shadow in the night. She slithered closer to Chandler like the serpent in the Garden. She remained calm and poised to strike. Chandler was focused on his mission and did not notice her approach.

“Chandler! Chandler, behind you!” Travis howled.

Chandler didn't look; he couldn't. He remained locked in on his objective. If his hand shook, the flame would waver and fall.

"Three seconds," Chandler announced.

Vale ripped free of Travis and stumbled forward, slower now and bleeding. For the first time since the demonstration, Vale was frightened. Travis shoved him back. Vale's eyes rolled into the back of his head as he spoke in Latin. To Chandler's surprise, Vale backed away. He turned, bolted out the door, and down the secret stairs, abandoning the heart of AI like a rat abandoning a sinking ship.

"He's... he's running away." Travis stared, unable to believe his own eyes.

"Five seconds! Six!" Chandler proclaimed.

The hum of the heart stopped. An eerie silence overcame the room. The AI bulbs went out and the hospital fell into complete darkness. Only the candle Chandler held remained, its flame illuminating the room.

"We did it." Travis let out a laugh.

Chandler exhaled, shaking. In the darkness, he heard someone ascending the stairs. The footsteps were controlled and measured, wraithlike. A voice echoed up the secret stairs.

"He's here," Vale called out, like a child announcing salvation. "He's here! He's here!"

The woman didn't move. She simply listened, as if she had been waiting for this moment. Footsteps reached the top of the stairs. A ghostly figure appeared in the doorway, backlit by a surreal light. The man wore a tattered uniform, his face bruised and his eyes black.

It was Pike or what was left of him! He was hunched over as though his movements were being guided by an unseen puppet marionette.

"That's not..." Travis was horrified.

"Madam," Pike smiled. This was not genuine. It was performance. "We have a security breach."

Vale had followed Pike and stood a few feet behind him at the top of the stairs. The woman turned and removed one of her gloves. Her expression softened to a smirk as she moved in one swift elegant motion. She placed her gloved hand on Pike's shoulder, like a loving mother to her child. Like a lover, her non-gloved hand rested on Vale's chest, and without a thought, she pushed.

Vale's feet slipped on the top step and his arms windmilled as he reached for a railing that wasn't there. He fell, tumbling down the secret staircase in a grotesque cascade, his limbs breaking. The sound of his body bounced, hitting wood, crunching with sickening thuds.

Pike froze, his mouth open, and joy filled his dead heart. He stared down the stairs as if he'd just watched the birth of a new era.

"Why?" yelled Chandler.

"Because... out with the old and in with the new," she purred, rubbing Pike's shoulder.

She instructed Pike to leave the hospital, whispering in his ear. Pike turned and walked down the stairs.

"It was you!" Travis barked, his chest heaving.

The woman looked at him as if he'd misunderstood the obvious. The flame of the candle shook slightly. Righteous anger pulsed through Travis's fists.

"You... you used Pike." Chandler seethed.

"You still don't see it," she said softly. "AI is wonderful news, right?" Her eyes slid to the candle, then to Chandler's face.

"Please stop saying that!" he demanded.

She took another step towards the candlelight. The warm glow painted her face into something almost human.

"Promising and remarkable," she echoed Chandler's own words he had said in the factory like she was quoting scripture. "You always choose the safest language, Chandler Bliss. You remain polite while the world changes around you."

Chandler did not respond. With the candle in his hand, he stepped closer to the heart, as his other hand reached for the nearest cable. Travis moved with him, grabbed a metal rod from the floor and lifted it like a hammer. They went to work, smashing the casing around the eye. The glass cracked and splintered like ice.

They pulled and snapped the cables. Each cable broke with sharp pops, releasing sparks and dying in the candlelight like flailing fireflies. Travis grunted with each strike, anger keeping him strong.

"More!" Chandler yelled. "Keep going!"

"You know," the woman watched, smiling and even clapping at times, "your grandfather understood change better than you do."

"Don't speak about him." Chandler's hands faltered, his rage surged.

"He wanted his factory first. He wanted AI first. He feared being outpaced." Her tone was amused. "Men like him always do. Too bad he will be unburdened soon enough!"

"Shut your mouth!" Travis raised the rod again.

"And yet you both think you're the heroes." The woman's smile sharpened.

Travis swung with fury, the rod smashing the main column with a loud clang. Something inside the column groaned and the metal bent as it stressed beyond its design. The heart's chamber shattered, and all six cables were destroyed beyond repair.

"We did it!" he exclaimed.

In the accompanying silence, a soft click sounded behind them, like a small device being primed. Chandler turned.

The woman moved silently towards them. She held something slim in her gloved hand. It was a doctor's tool, an injector, a polished instrument of death. Chandler tried to stop her, but he was not quick enough. She stepped in close and slipped under Travis's guard, driving the needle into his neck. Travis gasped and his eyes widened. His mouth opened as if to speak, but no words came as his knees buckled and he fell.

"Travis!" Chandler lunged. He tried to catch him, but Travis's body was too heavy and limp for Chandler to prevent a hard fall.

Travis's eyes locked on Chandler's, and he tried to smile. Chandler's world narrowed into a single point of horror.

"No," Chandler breathed. "No, no, you can't die!"

The woman stepped around them, her voice soft like a lullaby. "Don't you see? Humans are fragile."

Chandler snarled and surged to his feet. She was already moving again, flashing another syringe, the needle dripping with poison. Chandler threw his arm up, but it was too late. The sting hit the side of his arm. It was sharp and cold, as heat spread through his ribs like ink in water. His legs weakened and his vision blurred at the edges. He stumbled backwards, landing on the shattered casing of the heart. The candle fell from his hand, rolled, and settled upright miraculously, still burning.

Chandler collapsed on one knee, burning the image of the candle into his mind like it was the last honest thing left in Hanover.

The woman watched him with pity. "I asked you a question years ago," she said. "And you never answered it."

"I answered..." Chandler could barely speak.

"You didn't," she cut in, voice suddenly firm. "You dodged me with polite nonsense. You hid like a coward behind fear because you were afraid of losing your precious craft, your candles, and foolish nostalgia for the old world." She stepped closer, her face lit by the candle's wavering glow. "So, I'll ask you one more time."

Chandler looked up at her.

"AI is wonderful news, right?" Her voice was sweet and innocent, but dripped with venom.

Chandler tried to rise, but he couldn't. The poison had paralyzed most of his body. He turned away from her, dragging himself towards an open window with nothing but the remaining strength in his arms. He kept crawling towards it, each movement felt like pushing through mud.

He reached the window and gripped the sill with trembling hands. He hauled himself up, inch by inch, until he stood, swaying like a candle flame in a draft.

Outside, Hanover stretched beneath him. The skies were clear, and there was beautiful starlight illuminating the ground. For one brief, breathtaking moment, it looked like victory. The streets were alive with movement. People were running, not in terror, but in release. Doors were thrown open and families spilled into the night like water freed from a dam. He glimpsed a few candles on the horizon.

He saw Valerie and Kimberly below, guiding the freed prisoners out of captivity, their arms around shoulders, their voices raised in immense relief. He saw Earl Sr., candlemakers, lamplighters, and bakers, standing under the dead AI streetlamps, their faces tilted upward as if they were seeing stars again for the first time.

We did it, Chandler thought. He was dizzy with pain and his body was broken. He smiled as happy tears rolled down his cheeks. He cocked his head, hearing a gradual sound behind him. It was a rising hum that started small and grew to a howling greater than he had ever heard.

Chandler's smile faltered and his eyes darted toward the heart. The woman let out a diabolical laugh as she crushed the burning candle under her shoe. The hum swelled, returning like a resurrected curse. The overhead AI bulbs blinked on, and the hospital flooded with harsh white light, erasing shadows, erasing warmth and erasing the candle's heroism. Chandler's heart turned to despair.

"No," he whispered.

Behind him, the woman stood perfectly still. Her face was bathed in the returning AI glow like a saint in stained glass. She had not been afraid for she had known all along. Outside the window, on the streets below, Chandler saw movement shift, new figures emerging from alleys and doorways. It was Pike leading hundreds of Blueshirts who swung clubs, surrounding the escaping prisoners. Their batons caught the light and their eye-and-torch emblems gleamed. The prisoners were trapped!

The woman stepped closer, her voice near Chandler's ear. "Did you really think," she giggled, "something this beautiful could be amputated so easily?"

"You... Can't... Win..." Chandler turned to face her, his arms, paralyzed by his sides. "AI... Can't... Win...!"

"AI has already won! It's wonderful news, isn't it?" She kissed him on the forehead and shoved him out the window.

As he fell, the AI lights in Hanover returned. Street by street, the light regained control. Chandler fell through the light and into defeat. The last thing he saw, framed by the window like a perfect portrait, was the woman watching him die. All the while, the Blueshirts closed in on everyone he loved. Rae, the woman Chandler hoped to one day be the mother of his children, lay on the ground, lifeless.

Only the Beginning

Chandler woke up gasping. The room was dark, his sheets twisted around his legs, his heart pounding so hard it hurt. His pillow and mattress were coated in cold, nasty sweat. His thoughts were scattered as he tried to orient himself. The air smelled clean, too clean. There was no wax, no smoke, no scent except laundry detergent.

He sat up abruptly, pressing a hand to his shoulder. He ran his hands over his arms, his torso, and his palms. There was no apparent pain, numbness, or wires. A digital clock on the nightstand glowed: **7:41 A.M.** Chandler slowly swung his legs over the side of the bed and planted his feet on the floor. Carpet greeted him, soft and pleasant against his toes. The sun was shining through the window.

"What the heck?" he muttered. "A *nightmare*?"

The word felt borrowed the moment he said it, like something people used to make sense of impending doom. The horrors of Hanover hadn't faded the way dreams did. They weighed on his mind with clarity in images of the hospital lights, the hum beneath the city, Pike's eyes, and the moment the city went dark. He could still feel the burn in his nerves as he tried to gather himself. He jumped as the door creaked open.

"Hey, bro, you okay?" A man stepped inside.

He stood in the doorway wearing slacks and a polo shirt, hair still damp from the shower. A phone rested in one hand, a coffee mug in the other. His voice was friendly and cheerful.

"You were thrashing around like you were fighting someone," he said, tapping the light switch.

Chandler turned towards the door and looked around the room, trying to comprehend his surroundings. Posters lined the wall. A TV was mounted above a narrow dresser. The walls were painted a shark-colored gray, and in the corner sat a white laundry hamper with a broken handle. Overhead, a ceiling fan spun beneath four lights, surrounded by decorative glass fixtures. Then, he saw him.

"Pike!" Chandler hurled himself backward across the bed as if avoiding gunfire. "Get away from me!"

"Uh... okay." The man blinked. "When did we start calling each other by last names? Hey, Bliss, it's Monday, and you've got nineteen minutes... make that eighteen until we're both late."

"Yeah." Chandler forced himself to breathe. "Yeah, I'm coming, Henry. Sorry, bro. Bad dream."

“Figures,” Henry said, unconcerned. “Big day.”

“What?” Chandler asked.

“You forgot?” Henry grinned.

He crossed the room and tossed Chandler a clean shirt. Chandler caught it, instinctively, fingers closing around the fabric. Henry glanced at the bed, puzzled by the sheets torn from the corners, one pillow still in place, while the others lay scattered across the room.

“Late for what?” Chandler asked.

“Work, you know, the thing that pays all the bills. Hanover Technology Firm?” Henry raised an eyebrow.

The name landed like a punch to the gut as he remembered. Chandler looked around the room again. A framed college degree hung on the far side of the wall: **Bachelor’s in Software Engineering**. A bookshelf lined the wall, packed with manuals and code references. On the windowsill sat a single decorative candle, unlit. He was certain it had not been there before.

“Chandler?” Henry said, more cautiously.

“Yeah,” Chandler managed. “Yeah, sorry.”

Chandler stood and pulled the shirt over his shoulders, then stepped into his slacks and shoes as Henry headed back down the hall. In the mirror, Chandler caught his reflection. Everything felt wrong. His clothes were too clean. His teeth were too white. His face was smooth, clean-shaven.

There was no dirt beneath his fingernails. Chandler exited the room and hurried toward the door as Henry waited, checking his phone.

"Oh, don't forget your bag," Henry said, pointing to the shelf. "Mr. Pembroke, told us to bring our laptops for the demonstration today."

"What did you say?" Chandler froze at the threshold.

"Mr. Pembroke, our CEO," Henry spoke sarcastically. "He told us Friday he hired a new Director of Engineering Development. The whole company's meeting at noon. It's mandatory for all software developers. You always get like this before demos."

Chandler swallowed, grabbed his bag, and followed him out. Henry carried a sports jacket under his right arm, though the weather outside did not require it.

Outside, the city surged with motion. There were skyscrapers made of glass and steel touching the heavens. LED streetlights and screens glowed everywhere. There was light without flame. People moved quickly, eyes locked to devices, faces washed in white glare. Chandler and Henry walked a full block in silence.

"Hey, Henry," Chandler said suddenly. "Rae... she's still my girlfriend, right?"

Henry stopped midstride. "Uh, yeah? Chandler, you literally bought the ring last week."

"I did?" Chandler tried to catch his breath.

"Bro, you've been agonizing over how to propose. You and I sat for hours in the café on James Street yesterday while you rehearsed your speech. Dude, our buddy, Travis from Louisville, is ready to buy his plane ticket to come to the wedding."

"Yes! Right," Chandler replied. "Travis, our old friend, and Rae, my beautiful girlfriend."

"And rich, too," Henry laughed. "I wish my future father-in-law owned all the butcher shops on the east coast. Her dad, Earl, is worth millions! Cha-ching!"

"Hey, Henry, you ever get the feeling you've lived something before?" Chandler exhaled and looked up at the streetlights, perfect, seamless.

"Like déjà vu?" Henry shrugged. "Like when you already know how the movie ends?"

Chandler didn't answer. It didn't matter anyway. They'd reached the building at **8:01.** The receptionist, Miss Leslie, greeted them both by name. Henry peeled off toward his office. Chandler made his way to his office trying to experience normalcy as much as possible.

At noon, Chandler sat in the auditorium, hands folded, heart racing. Every department was there. The room darkened, as a curtain hiding the screen fell away with a heavy swoosh. The CEO stepped onto the stage.

"Good afternoon," he said. "Today, I want to show you something that's going to change everything. Something that will make you more efficient, more productive, and most importantly, something you will love."

The screen behind him glowed with bright colors. Chandler's fingers curled into his palms and he felt nauseous. Somewhere deep inside him, beneath logic, beneath code, beneath the comfort of forgetting, a flame stirred. This was all too familiar.

At the CEO's signal, a confident man with a practiced smile, took the podium and loaded a page with a search bar at its center. As the screen refreshed, a familiar shape flashed. It was ringed like a pupil, bright, with a flame at the center, gone before Chandler could focus on it.

The CEO announced, "The future of software development is here." The room went silent and Chandler nearly fell from his chair. At once, the applause came, accompanied by a standing ovation. The CEO shook hands with investors. Board members discussed large compensation packages and profitability.

Departments buzzed with plans, how they'd use it, how it would help. They called it a gift, a miracle, and a blessing. Leaders patted their teams on the shoulders, praising better efficiency, productivity, and a better work-life balance.

To Chandler's horror, a part of him understood why everyone was excited. And then, he saw her. The mysterious woman stepped forward and whispered into the new Director's ear. She addressed the room, voice soft and assured, and spoke into the microphone.

"It's wonderful news, right?" Her eyes found Chandler's and she winked.

Chandler looked at Pike, who had put on his blue sports jacket. Chandler realized he'd been wrong...

The nightmare wasn't over;
it had simply found a future!

The Appendices

A Brief History of Light in Hanover

1676 – The First Communal Chandlery
A shared candle house is established near the riverbank. Families contribute rendered tallow in exchange for allotted tapers. Excess burning is publicly discouraged and waste is fined.

1684 – The Lamplighter's Walk
Hanover appoints its first official lamplighter. A single nightly route is established, lighting posts near the Covenant Cathedral, river crossing, and market square. The walk becomes a symbol of safety and civic order.

1690 – Standardization of the Hanover Taper
Candlemakers agree upon a city-standard taper length and burn time. This allows churches, taverns, and city guards to plan evenings with consistent and predictable burn times.

1701 – The Founding of the Candlemakers' Guild
Apprenticeships become formalized. Ritual handwashing before work is recorded for the first time, noted as "readiness of both hand and mind."

1728 – The Great Winter Shortage
A harsh winter strains supplies. Candles are rationed. Citizens gather earlier in the evenings. Crime drops noticeably, later cited as evidence by Sullivan Vale that reducing candles is the best route to ensure safety.

1759 – Expansion of Street Lamps
Lamp posts are extended into residential streets. Hanover increases taxes to cover the costs. Children grow accustomed to seeing fire carried gently through the night.

1784 – Fire on James Street
A residence fire claims several homes. In response, candle holders are redesigned, chimneys improved, and wax blends refined. The city chooses adaptation over abandonment of flame.

1812 – Introduction of Industrial Candle Production
Larger factories appear, though most remain family-run. Candlemakers argue that speed without care produces sloppy candles.

1831 – The Age of Candlelight Named
The phrase "Age of Candlelight" appears in print in the Hanover Journal. The editorial infers that one day a new source of light will be available, which will end the age.

1849 – The Gaslight Riots
A proposal in City Hall introducing gas lighting is debated and ultimately declined due to safety concerns and loss of local trades. The Bliss Family is the main opponent of the initiative.

1867 – Candlemakers' Jubilee
The city honors candlemakers with a public ceremony. Earl Bliss Sr. is given the "Keys to Hanover" for his dedication to Hanover.

1879 – The First Reports of 'Unreliable Candles'
The Hanover Journal publishes an article describing Hanover's streets as "poorly lit," despite no recorded changes in candle quantity or quality. Public perception quietly shifts.

1884 – The Demonstration
Artificial Illumination is unveiled at City Hall. Candles are not extinguished that day, but something colder replaces them. For the first time in Hanover's history, the candlemakers' days are numbered.

*The Apostasia Pyros Speech

Delivered by: Director Sullivan Vale

October 31, 1885

Before you speak another word. Before you shout my name like a bark you think has teeth, let us be clear about how you arrived here. You did not wake up one morning and build a city. Mayor Pembroke did!

When Hanover was choking on soot and meandering on dim streets, when crime hid comfortably in shadows, when businesses fled to brighter cities, Pembroke made the decision that no one else was brave enough to make. He *invited* ***me***! Not you, not the guilds, not the trades, and certainly not the Bliss family.

It was me. He brought me here when this city was stagnant, when your "traditions" were bleeding it dry with the inefficient ways of old. He gave me authority because authority was required. And together, we delivered results.

Let us review them since memory grows selective when fear sets in. Street crime fell. Productivity rose. Factories expanded. Investment returned. Insurance rates dropped. Night became usable. That was not because of wax. That was not because of flame. That was because of policy, and policy has a name. Vale!

You speak as though something was taken from you as though you were robbed. No, you were simply outgrown and diminished. Every improvement you now enjoy, every safer street, every longer workday, every merchant who stayed instead of leaving, exists because I intervened.

Not because you asked, but because you could not. And now you stand before me and dare to suggest that nothing I have done was for you? Nothing? Then tell me. Who paid you while production was cut? Who converted your contracts instead of tearing them up? Who prevented your workshops from being closed? Who ensured your children still ate while your relevance expired?

It was not the flame that gave you salvation. It was me. Let me correct a misunderstanding. You are not owed traditions. You are not owed respect. You are not owed a future that looks like your past. You are owed order, and order has been delivered to you by me.

Artificial Illumination was not created to honor you. It was created to replace you when necessary, and you have the nerve to think you should get to decide when that is? You lacked discipline and you were inefficient. If that offends you, understand this: being offended is a luxury of the powerful, and you are no longer powerful. You will adapt, or you will diminish. This is not a threat; it is a guaranteed outcome.

Pembroke understood the simplicity of this. He understood that leadership means choosing who the city is for and who it must leave behind. He chose progress and so did I.

Now, I order you to stand in the light I have given you or step aside and stop blocking it. History will move either way. It is your choice!

The Candlemaker's Glossary

(*As Used in Hanover*, 1884)

Apprentice
A learner bound by contract to an expert candlemaker, typically for a term of five to seven years.

Beeswax
A superior candle material produced by honeybees. Burns cleaner and longer than tallow, with a natural scent. Reserved for churches, formal homes, and ceremonial use due to cost.

Burn Time
The measured time a candle is expected to produce steady flame under normal conditions. A well-made taper burns evenly without excessive smoke.

Chandlery
A workshop or establishment where candles are made, stored, and sold. In Hanover, the term often refers to the Bliss Candle Factory.

Cooling Rack
Wooden or iron frames where newly formed candles are hung or laid to cool and harden. Rushing this process results in warping or cracking.

Curing
The period during which finished candles are left undisturbed. This allows the wax and wick to fully settle. Candles that are not properly cured are prone to uneven burning.

Dip / Dipping
A traditional method of candlemaking in which wicks are repeatedly dipped into molten wax until the desired thickness is achieved.

Draft
Air movement that affects flame behavior. A skilled candlemaker accounts for drafts when testing burn quality. A candle that fails in calm air is considered poorly made.

Flame Breathing
An informal term used by candlemakers to describe how a flame responds to nearby motion, breath, or passing air.

Guttering
The running or dripping of melted wax down the side of a candle, usually caused by improper wick sizing or poor wax blend.

Hand-Finished
A candle shaped, smoothed, and trimmed by hand after molding or dipping. Considered a mark of quality and pride.

Industrial Candle
Large, thick candles designed for factories, mines, and street lamps. Built for longevity and resilience rather than elegance.

Lamplighter
A contracted municipal worker responsible for lighting, tending, and extinguishing street lamps.

Mold
A metal or wooden form into which molten wax is poured. Mold-cast candles are uniform but require hand finishing to ensure quality.

Ritual Wash
The practice of washing hands before beginning work. Chandler and many others do this not for cleanliness alone, but to signal readiness and respect for the craft.

Snuffing
Extinguishing a flame by cutting off its air supply, rather than blowing. Considered proper form and believed to preserve wick integrity.

Steady Flame
A flame that burns upright, calm, and without excessive flicker. The hallmark and guarantee of a Bliss product.

Tallow
Rendered animal fat used in most everyday candles. Affordable and widely available, though prone to smoke and odor if poorly prepared.

Taper
A slender candle, narrower at the top than the base. Commonly used in homes, churches, and hand-held holders.

Wick
The braided or twisted fiber at the center of a candle that draws melted wax upward to sustain flame. Wick quality determines burn behavior.

Wick Trimming
The practice of cutting a wick to proper length before lighting. Prevents smoke, popping, and uneven burning. Apprentices are trained to perform this task first.

Wax Blend
The specific mixture of materials used in candlemaking. The Bliss Family recipe is a guarded family secret.

Wind-Test
An informal test in which a candle is exposed to light air movement to judge flame resilience. A candle meant for street use must pass this test.

This book ends here. If you choose to leave an honest review on Amazon, thank you!

www.ingramcontent.com/pod-product-compliance
Lightning Source LLC
La Vergne TN
LVHW031925090826
845145LV00018B/2833

* 9 7 8 1 9 4 9 4 3 9 2 0 5 *